Wishing Joy

by

JoMarie DeGioia

PUBLISHED BY:

Bailey Park Publishing

I0545748

Wishing Joy

Book Ten of the
Cypress Corners Series

by

JoMarie DeGioia

Chapter 1

Cypress Corners, Florida

"It's a great offer, Zach." Zach Harris's brother Chase leaned back, crossing his arms. "If you take it, you won't have to buy me out."

Zach squinted down at the papers spread out over the wrought iron tabletop as the chilly breeze fluttered their edges. He read the numbers easily enough, but the words seemed to swim so he chose to ignore them at the moment.

He faced his brother again. "I'm not sure if I'm selling the ranch, Chase."

Chase gaped at him. Zach could see where he was coming from. The family ranch had been a sore subject between the brothers for years now, even before their father died almost eighteen months ago. Wild Harry Harris hadn't been a warm or caring father, but he'd taken care of the land, the herd and the horses. As for his sons and their cousin Billy? They were left pretty much on their own.

"Dude, the place is dragging you down."

Zach snorted. "You used to want to be a part of it. Before Dad died."

Chase shrugged. "Maybe. Since then, I've learned that life

is too damn short to worry over the old man's approval."

Zach blinked. Sure, Chase had a different perspective now. He was married, to a girl he met at their cousin Billy's wedding on New Year's Eve. Chase was a father now himself, actually. Zach's little niece was almost two months old already. As for Billy, he and his wife Shannon had begun to build a life here in Cypress. Chase and his family had settled here too, temporarily at least, until Zach found the money to buy him out of his half of the ranch.

"Are you going to get a house here in Cypress, then?" Zach asked.

Chase grinned. "I just might, if I have enough liquid assets."

Zach found a smile of his own. "I'll think about it, bro. That's the best I can do right now. Okay?"

Chase came to his feet and turned, settling his hands on the back of his chair. "Why don't you come over tomorrow for Thanksgiving?"

"Out in Cypress? Don't tell me you're still staying at the tent-cabin."

"No way. We outgrew that little love shack once Caitlyn came along."

Caitlyn, that adorable little bun who was in the oven when Chase and Carrie got married.

"She didn't take very long, either," Zach said.

Chase threw his head back and laughed. "Timing is everything, bro. Nah, I meant Billy and Shannon's place."

Zach scratched his chin. "Their house is finished?"

"Just about. I've been helping him out with some of the finish stuff. Moldings. Painting. That kind of thing. The house is plenty ready enough to slap on the feedbag."

Zach felt like a dick. He hadn't even realized that Billy's house was ready to be occupied, not that he'd kept up with the latest on either his brother or their cousin.

"I don't think so."

"What are you going to do instead?" Chase smirked at him. "Eat alone at the ranch house?"

Zach just shrugged.

Chase looked like he was going to say something else, but he just gave a curt nod. "You have my number if you change your mind. Or hell, just drop by. Billy said Shannon is making a ton of food. I think her sister's family is coming, too."

Zach didn't know Shannon very well, let alone her sister. "I'll think about it."

With that, Chase left Zach sitting alone at his table.

Zach rubbed a hand over his face. Maybe he should get the hell out of the ranch. It didn't hold any fond memories for him. That was for sure. Their mother had left when he was ten, never to be heard from again. Their father, always the strong silent type, had all but withdrawn into himself after she'd run off with that equipment salesman.

When Billy had come to live with them a couple of years later, not a one of them had made a real place for him. The old man's stoicism had lasted until he got sick and never told his family. Lung cancer, a surprise for a guy who might have looked like the Marlboro man but had never smoked a cigarette in his life. He'd left a fortune to their cousin, though. Surprising the hell out of Billy and pissing off Chase but good. Zach hadn't really cared. He had enough to worry about without harboring any resentment over his father's money.

Wild Harry Harris hadn't shown any more affection toward Billy than he had to Chase and Zach. That didn't stop Zach from missing his father. He pushed the thought aside, like he usually did. Turning melancholy over all they could have had as a family made him feel like a pathetic little pussy.

A memory tickled at the back of his mind. Something

about a Christmas at the ranch before their mother left. A huge tree in the living room. A big wreath on the front door. He shoved the memory aside. It was probably just wishful thinking on his part. He didn't think his mother had ever been happy on the ranch. Why the hell would she have made a happy holiday for her sons?

The courtyard of the coffee shop was all decked out for the holiday, with paper turkeys and horns-o-plenty stuck everywhere. Acorns and pumpkins and artificial leaves were thrown around to mix with the giant brown leaves from the Sycamores towering overhead. If he recalled correctly from a visit to Cypress about a year ago, Christmas decorations would take over before tomorrow's turkey was eaten.

Cypress was an anomaly, sitting on over ten thousand acres of the prettiest land in Central Florida with about seventy percent of it set aside for conservation of native plants and animals. Zach knew it had once been a ranch over ten times the size of theirs, and in the wilder parts you could see where cattle had formed rutted paths over the scrub and sand for generations.

The town had been developed over fifteen years ago, but appeared older and more established. It featured upscale retail, state-of-the-art homes and an award-winning golf course. Then there was the homey small-town square. Things were pretty quiet now that the bakery and coffee shop were closed for the night. Most of the folks in St. Cloud referred to Cypress as Stepford. It did look pretty damn perfect, and the town square looked like something from out of a movie.

The breeze kicked up, rustling the few remaining Sycamore leaves overhead. Zach stood and grabbed his leather jacket. Central Florida's hotter than Hell summers and surprisingly cold if short-lived winters were something he'd grown up with. It felt a little chillier out here than it did in the city. Or on the ranch, for that matter.

Both his brother and his cousin seemed to really like the place. Billy and his wife were settled in their farmhouse and busy setting up their goat farm and petting zoo. Chase seemed to have made up for his shitty treatment of Billy when they were kids, seeing as now he happily worked with him.

Zach nodded absently at an older couple walking by as he headed to his truck. His night was wide open. He could stop at the End Zone sports bar in St. Cloud and pick up a game of pool or a quick lay, but he wasn't really in the mood for either. He sure as hell wouldn't think about holidays past or even present tonight. He was alone. And once he either bought Chase out of the ranch or sold the damn thing, that would become a permanent situation.

And no amount of turkey or Christmas candy would change that for him.

***

"You've got to be kidding me." Joy Rollins stood at the top of the stairs of the Cypress Inn, her hands on her hips. Christmas music rang from every corner of the lobby and the banister of the curved staircase was wrapped with faux greenery. "It's barely Thanksgiving, Mom."

Her mother, the proud owner of the Cypress Corners bed and breakfast, clicked her tongue as she tweaked a big red velvet bow tied around the newel post. "Our critically-acclaimed Thanksgiving brunch is over, Joy. I want to get a jump on the season."

The woman was certainly getting a jump on things, all right. A ruffled apron covered with candy canes was tied around her compact body and her salt and red-pepper hair was pulled back in a bun. She had a real Mrs. Claus thing going, if Santa's wife was in her early fifties.

Joy rolled her eyes and took plodding steps down the stairs. "Can't all this wait until Saturday?"

Karen Rollins gave her oldest child a look Joy had seen too many times in her life. "The decorations have to go up, dear. And lots of them. The inn must look like a winter wonderland."

Joy didn't bother to argue the point as she ducked into the kitchen to grab a bottle of pinot from the butler's pantry. The absurd idea of a winter wonderland in Central Florida was a subject she wouldn't broach today.

The inn was the picture of Old Florida, with plastered walls, thick square columns and potted palms tucked in every corner. *Those poor palms.* They had no idea what they were in for. They'd be all but strangled in twinkly lights before the day was out.

In the twelve years the B and B had been in business, her mother had gone all out every Christmas. Her parents had built the inn and then, soon after it opened, a massive heart attack had taken her father right out of the Christmas card picture. Joy had been fifteen, and very close to her dad.

Their dad had loved the holidays, though. He would have jumped right into the decorating alongside their mom.

Joy swallowed past the lump in her throat. Her dad had died in the summer but she thought about him more and more once Thanksgiving gave way to Christmas every year. It was her favorite time of the year too, not that she'd admit that to her mother on Thanksgiving day.

"I'm going to the tavern to meet up with Becky and Jessie."

Her sister Becky had recently escaped the inn and lived over in a two-bedroom near the town center.

"Is Jessie making dinner this year?" her mother asked.

"No. Her sister is."

"Out at that pretty farmhouse?"

Joy nodded. Billy and Shannon's place beside their goat farm and petting zoo was very pretty, and just about finished.

"You're taking a bottle of wine?" Her mother shook her head. "I would think they would appreciate something from Sweet Escape. Or some of our famous cinnamon rolls."

"The bakery is closed today, Mom. I'm sure Caro is enjoying her holiday with her husband and baby. As to the cinnamon rolls? I doubt there are any left from brunch."

Her mother flashed a smile. "There aren't." She sighed. "Then I guess it will just be me and Tom today."

Joy caught the wistfulness in her mother's voice. Tom, the youngest Rollins, would probably be anywhere his latest crush was. Last she'd heard he had it bad for Ashlyn, the girl who worked at Sweet Escape with Caro Graham. He was a good guy, though. He'd show up if their mom called. *Better him than me.*

"Okay then, I'll see you later."

Joy kissed her mother on the cheek and started to make her way through the lobby.

"Don't forget about the photo op on Saturday," her mother called over her shoulder.

Joy froze, her hand on the scrolled brass handle. "Oh God, no. Not the photo op."

"Joy, it's been a staple at the inn for years."

Joy turned and smirked in her direction. "Years?"

"All right, since last year. The reception was dynamic, though. I want to build on that."

"And?"

Her mother sniffed and gave a nod. "And I want to beat the town square to the punch."

"There isn't a photo op in the town square."

"No, but residents and visitors like to take their Christmas card photos on the gazebo."

"It's picturesque."

"Not as much as our inn, Joy. The Cypress Inn has character." She winked. "In more ways than one."

Joy just sighed. "I'll see you later, Mom."

She stepped outside and took in a breath. There was a decidedly chill in the air at last. She wore dark jeans cuffed at the ankles paired with a thin V-neck sweater in her favorite shade of mossy green. Tan suede booties with thick wooden heels finished what she considered a Thanksgiving-appropriate outfit, and her hair was in long loose waves instead of the ponytail she usually wore. Becky and their brother Tom both shared their mother's red hair while Joy had what her mother called chestnut and Joy thought of as brown.

She'd grown up in Florida, to the east in Melbourne. Her parents had bought in to the whole Cypress experience from the jump. The nature. The animals. The way of living. It hadn't exactly sucked for Joy and her siblings, moving to Cypress in its early days. Going to a brand new high school had been nice, since everyone in her class had also been the "new kid."

She walked to her car, eyeing its dusty appearance with a sigh. Her Jeep wasn't anything like Jessie's pink cutie. No, the red paint on Joy's Jeep was faded and its black top was starting to crack. Heck, it had been gently used when she'd bought it.

She'd taken it with her to the University of Central Florida for her freshman year, and then back to UCF for grad school after taking a gap year to figure out just what she would do with her Bachelor's Degree in Art. And then she'd crammed it full of her few belongings when she'd quit after two years and returned home to Cypress seven months ago. She hadn't created a darn thing since the day she'd moved back, either.

She ignored the squeak of her driver's side door as she opened it, got behind the wheel and set the wine bottle on the passenger seat. The parking lot of the tavern was almost empty when she got there, no real surprise since the place had closed at three today. Her sister Becky stood with Jessie near Noah's quad-cab truck. A little tow-headed boy, Jessie's stepson Max, stood with his dad. Noah was as blond as his little boy, and dressed in what Joy figured was dress casual. Chinos and a blue chambray shirt, a grown-up version of his son's outfit.

Becky waved as Joy parked and turned off the engine. Aside from hair color, the sisters looked a lot alike. They both had big brown eyes and stood five foot four in bare feet.

"Hey, sis." Becky hugged her. "How's Mom today?"

Joy let out a breath. "In full holiday mode."

Becky's eyes widened. "Man, I'm glad I don't live there anymore."

"Traitor." Joy laughed. "Do you need a roommate?"

"Are you serious?"

"I'd love to get out of the inn but you're just getting settled. It's only been a couple of months since you moved out."

Becky shrugged. "I'd make room for my big sis."

Joy's throat tightened. Becky was barely one year younger than Joy at twenty-five, yet she seemed to have her life on track. Joy wouldn't do anything to throw a roadblock in her way. Her aimless big sister barreling in on her independence? Yeah. That would be one big-ass roadblock.

"Thanks, but I'll survive," Joy said.

The sisters both greeted Jessie and her little family, and then Noah lifted his chin toward a six-seater electric golf cart parked at the curb. "We're taking the Gator."

The vehicle was one that the Cypress Institute liked to use for eco-tours and to take prospective residents and visitors to the wilder side of Cypress. The fat nubby tires bounced the cart over the rough-in-spots road out to the east side of the property and the open sides let the chilled breeze run through. Little Max chattered away from his spot next to Becky, while Joy nodded and tried not to feel like excess baggage all alone in the back seat.

As they rounded a bend to the right, the petting zoo and

farmhouse came into view. To Joy it looked rustic yet pretty, and the little goats prancing around behind the ranch fencing gave the place a real country feel. She knew that Ben Chapman had designed it to Billy's specifications, and that Noah had built most of it.

When Noah stopped the cart, the others all got out and made their way up to the wide front door. Joy followed, considerably more slowly. Why had she agreed to come to this family thing?

Because the alternative is stringing Christmas lights and garland all over the inn.

A truck even bigger than Noah's pulled into the drive and a tall guy stepped out. He looked a lot like Billy and Chase Harris, with sun-streaked brown hair and broad shoulders. His long legs were clad in dark jeans and he wore an open blue flannel shirt over a gray Henley. He appeared to be hanging back as well, holding on to the opened door of his truck and staring up at the farmhouse. He looked about as uncomfortable as she felt, even if he was still the hottest guy she'd seen in forever with that slight frown on his face.

Joy worked in the hospitality business, didn't she? She'd been raised to be accommodating hadn't she? Her father had always said that she could make the Mona Lisa grin.

Her pulse gave a jump as she approached mister tall, dark and brooding. Maybe he was a lost cause. She might be clueless. Aimless. A cockeyed optimist.

But she was never one to back down from a challenge.

Chapter 2

Zach tightened his grip on the edge of the truck door, and then forced himself to loosen his grasp. Why the hell had he agreed to come to this family thing?

Chase had called this morning and Zach just couldn't think of another excuse to avoid it, that was why. At least he hadn't pushed Zach for his decision on the sale of the ranch. And Zach doubted his brother would bring up the prickly subject with so many people around.

He took in a breath and slowly let it out.

"Hey, there," a woman said from behind him.

He turned and found a pretty brunette smiling up at him. "Hey, yourself."

"Let me guess," she said. "Excess baggage?"

"Huh?"

"You. Here on your own. Believe me, I feel for you."

He found a smile for her. "I guess that's one way to put it." He dipped his head. "Zach Harris."

"Joy Rollins." Her deep brown eyes widened a fraction. "Wait. Harris? Like Billy and Chase?"

"Yep. My cousin and brother."

She cocked her head to one side, her wavy hair catching

the afternoon light with chestnut streaks he'd missed at first. "Hmm." She cradled the wine bottle she carried in one arm. "I've heard of the elusive Harris."

"That would be me."

Her full lips curved in a wide smile. He ran his eyes over her again. That soft green sweater did something to her curves as the V dipped between what he could guess were prime tits, and her jeans were dark and fitted to a pair of shapely legs. She was lean and curvy, and would probably be a nice little distraction from the shit-fest that was his life right now.

"And just what do you know about excess baggage?" he asked.

"You're looking at a fellow fifth wheel."

She sure didn't look like a party crasher. "You weren't invited?"

She nodded. "I was. I'm a friend of Shannon's sister."

She was a friend of his cousin's sister-in-law. That might be a little too close for comfort. No matter how she was affecting him, she might be a distraction he should avoid.

"Well, friend of Shannon's sister, let's get inside and get this over with."

She snorted a sweet little laugh. "Happy Thanksgiving, I

guess."

He waved her in front of him. As she passed him on her way to the front porch, she left the scent of something sweet and hot in her wake. He couldn't quite place it, but it made his belly clench. The sight of her fine ass in those jeans wasn't bad either.

There was a bunch of women crowded into the entry of Billy's house, but he spotted his cousin not far behind his wife.

"Hey, cuz," Billy said.

"Hey, Billy."

The cute little blond at Billy's elbow smiled at him. "I'm so glad you decided to come, Zach."

"Thanks for having me, Shannon."

He noticed then that several people had brought bottles of wine, like the brunette, or bakery boxes and he stood there with empty hands. He clenched and unclenched them at his sides.

The rest of them continued talking as Shannon led everybody into the big kitchen at the back of the house. The place did look nearly complete, and the thick moldings and wide plank floor gave it a real welcoming feel. It was nothing like the oversized house at the ranch.

Zach hung back again. Chase caught his eye and raised a brow in Joy's direction. He must have seem them come in together. Zach wouldn't take the bait, though.

The smell of turkey filled the house and Zach's stomach gave a rumble. Chase came up to him and handed him a beer.

"I'm glad you came, bro."

Zach nodded. "Thanks. Why didn't you tell me to bring something?"

"Like what?"

"Cake or flowers or something."

Chase blinked at him. "I don't know."

Zach guessed that had they been brought up by their mother, or at least a father who gave a shit, maybe the Harris boys would have known some of the social niceties, like not showing up at a party emptyhanded.

"I'm sure Billy and Shannon don't care." Chase stepped closer. "So what's with you and the cute brunette?"

"What do you mean?"

Chase raised both brows this time. "She's hot, man. And I'm speaking as a happily married man. Completely objective."

"I just walked in with her, Chase. I don't know her."

"You don't know who?" Carrie said as she came to stand with her husband. She kissed Zach's cheek and stepped back. "Hi, Zach."

"Hi, Carrie."

Chase put an arm around Carrie's shoulder and dropped a kiss on her strawberry hair. "Zach here doesn't know Becky's sister."

"Joy?" Carrie broke out in a smile. "Oh, I love Joy!"

Zach noticed that several pairs of eyes were turned in their direction. His cheeks heated and he shoved his hands in his pockets. "How's that little carrottop, Carrie?"

"Taking a nap, thank God." Carrie rolled her eyes. "She doesn't know which is day and which is night yet."

"She will, baby." Chase rubbed Carrie's shoulder. "You'll see."

Carrie slanted a look at Zach and laughed at Chase. "Okay, big daddy."

Chase growled playfully at his wife and Zach took that as his cue to make himself scarce. This was going to be a long damn day. He made his way into the family room, his gaze running over the beamed ceiling and stacked stone fireplace. Billy and Shannon could use some more furniture, though. Maybe some of the stuff out at the ranch could work for them. If Zach ended up selling? He'd have a shit ton of stuff to get rid of.

The big flat-screen above the fireplace was pretty nice,

though. And the wide leather sofa, too.

He smiled absently at a tall blond guy and his gaze fell on the short-haired woman seated beside him on that sofa. She brightened, and waved.

"Hi, Zach. I'm Jessie." When Zach just stared at her she went on. "Shannon's sister."

"Nice to meet you," he said with a nod.

"Noah Brady," the blond guy said, holding out his hand.

Zach shook it. "Nice to meet you, Noah."

"Wow, you look a lot like your brother," Jessie said. "You and Billy Goat are obviously family, too."

Zach chuckled at his cousin's nickname. "I guess there's no mistaking a Harris man. You and your sister are two peas in a pod, for sure."

Jessie grinned. Zach had never met Shannon's sister before, but there was no denying their connection. Shannon's blond hair was longer than Jessie's short cut, but their bright eyes and wide smiles were identical. A little boy came up and bounced onto the couch beside Jessie.

"Max, this is Zach," she said.

The little boy stared at him and then nodded. "Hi, Zach."

"Hey."

Zach had little else to say to him. He wasn't around kids much, but he guessed that might change as Chase's daughter got older. And maybe Billy and Shannon would have a kid soon, too. Once he'd thought maybe he'd have a kid or two by now, he was thirty-one already, but that was a tough thing to pull off when you never dated. No expectations beyond a good time was pretty much his playbook. Why put stock in anything else?

Suddenly the room felt too hot. Too close. He came to his feet, nodded at the Brady family and stepped into the kitchen. Shannon and Carrie were busy, along with a redhead who looked a lot like his brunette. He inwardly winced. *The* brunette. Joy.

"Zach, do you know Becky?" Shannon asked.

Zach shook his head and smiled at the redhead. "Zach Harris."

"Hi, Zach Harris." The redhead grinned. "So how do you know my sister?"

Zach blinked and his sister-in-law laughed. "Zach doesn't know Joy, Becky," Carrie said. "At least that's what Chase said."

"I just walked in with her," he said again.

The three women exchanged some kind of silent girl-speak before Billy's wife seemed to take pity on him.

26

"It's almost time to eat, Zach," Shannon told him. "Why don't you head over to the table?"

Zach took the out she gave him and hightailed it out of there. The big farmhouse table was set for a lot of people and the curvy brunette was there already. She was seated about halfway down the table, her chin resting in her cupped hand. Her brow was furrowed and if he had to put a name to the expression on her face he would have to call it lonely.

He cleared his throat and she turned her head to face him. And then she smiled.

***

Dinner was delicious, but the wine was even better. Joy slowly twirled the stem of her glass on the tall counter where she sat perched on a comfy stool. Conversation had bounced all around her during dinner. She'd kept up her end of things, like a true Rollins. Now she happily sipped a glass of pinot much better than the one she'd brought and enjoyed the relative quiet of the kitchen as the sounds of chatter and football drifted over from the great room. She had a small plate of fig slices and goat cheese made from the milk of those little furry cuties out front, and she took a nibble of both.

She'd managed to ignore the pointed glances from both

27

Carrie and Becky across the big farmhouse table during dinner, too. Clearly, they wondered what was up with her and Zach. She could tell them easily enough, if she wanted to put them out of their misery. There was *nothing* there, but Joy wouldn't tell them that. Let they plot and plan. Joy wasn't going to throw herself at Zach Harris just because he looked like he was more than able to catch her.

"Not a football fan?" Zach asked as he stepped into the kitchen.

Joy let her gaze run over him nice and slow for one long minute. Now that she'd had the chance to stare at him a little bit, he'd sat nearly across from her at dinner after all, she could see more differences between him and the other Harris men.

He was just as tall and broad, had the same thick messy waves and dusting of stubble over his chiseled jaw, but his eyes were a gorgeous shade of blue she'd never seen before on a guy. Something between lapis and cobalt. The artist in her appreciated the handsome symmetry of his face. And his lips were full and surprisingly sensual. Those lips curved at one side in an almost-smile.

"You should try that more often," she said.

"What?"

"Smiling."

Something flickered in his eyes. "Can't help smiling with Joy."

That surprised a laugh out of her. "Still waters, Zach. That's what you are."

He shrugged and sat down next to her. "Around here, that could be dangerous."

"Are you talking about alligators?" She shook her head and took another sip of wine. "I'm not worried about them."

"Why not?"

"I know how to look out for them." She turned and leaned an elbow on the counter. "Didn't you grow up around here?"

"Over in St. Cloud, yeah." He folded his arms, he had some nice arms, and leaned closer. "Not many gators on the ranch, though."

"So you have horses and stuff?"

He chuckled, the sound a little rusty. "And stuff, yeah."

"I've never ridden a horse."

"We'll have to fix that."

Joy's belly dipped and she held up her hands. "No thanks."

"Are you afraid of horses?"

"Not afraid, exactly." She shrugged. "Let's just say I have

a healthy respect for them."

He took a piece of goat cheese from her plate and popped it in his mouth, chewing thoughtfully for a minute. "I take it you're not afraid of the little critters here on the farm?"

"Who could be afraid of them?"

His eyes sparkled then, adding an interesting element to his crooked smile. "You've never come across a buck, then."

"I don't know." She couldn't help but flirt back, if only to see more of that sparkle in those pretty eyes of his. "Have I?"

He barked out a laugh then, surprising in its lightness. "Not touching that one."

"So you're a rancher? A real rancher?"

"Yep. What do you do?"

"Anything and everything."

His eyes narrowed a little. "That's a loaded answer."

She took a breath and began her litany of odd-jobs she filled in Cypress. "I work at the Town Tavern a few days a week."

"Bartender?"

"Nope. Hostess. Waitress." That sounded lame, even to her. "I fill in for Becky at the Cypress Institute when she has to go up to Orlando for the director now and then. I'm also a substitute teacher at the community school. Then, of course, there's working at the Cypress Inn. For my mother."

He dipped his head. "Sounds like you keep busy."

"And she's only going to get busier," Becky announced as she breezed into the kitchen.

Zach arched a brow and faced Joy's sister. "What's that mean?"

Joy shook her head. "Never mind."

"Big sis here is going to join our mother's yearly holiday extravaganza this year," Becky said.

Joy's face heated as she tried to laugh it off. "It's no biggie."

"Don't tell Mom that," Becky said.

"Your mother's holiday what?" Zach asked.

Joy shot her sister a pointed look and waved her hand. "Our mother goes all out at the inn for Christmas. We're expected to participate."

He gave a slow nod. "I came to one of the holiday festivals out here last year. I couldn't believe the way Stepford throws itself into the whole shebang."

"Don't let any of the residents hear you call Cypress that." Becky laughed. "If Cypress tries to be perfect, that's only magnified during the holidays."

"I never really saw the point of going all out," he said. "It's just a day, after all."

Joy gaped at him. She could hear her sister suck in a breath behind her.

"Just a day?" Joy asked. "Look, I might not want to string twinkly lights and holly on every vertical surface in Cypress but Christmas is not just a day."

That sadness came into Zach's pretty eyes again. "It is to me."

Whoa. His voice was flat and his mouth set in a line. Joy had a flash of clarity in that moment. As hot and interesting as this guy was? He was too deep in himself to ever be more than a passing flirtation.

For some reason, that seemed to suck the energy right out of her.

Chapter 3

"Candy canes." Joy blew out a breath and tugged on the silly green pointy shoes. "Candy canes?"

"Yes, dear," her mother called from all the way out in the kitchen. "Candy canes."

Joy straightened. Jeez, the woman had ears like a bat. She walked back to the kitchen, the bells on her skirt jingling the whole while.

"Mom, you can't seriously expect me to brave a certain big-box store on Black Friday."

"I do." Her mother's face held a soft smile. "Remember how much your father loved braving the crowds, Joy?"

Joy did. "He called it going on the hunt."

They shared a laugh. "So do your father's memory proud and bring us back one hundred and fifty boxes of candy canes."

Joy gaped at her. "How many?"

"That's just to get us started. Oh, and more twinkly lights."

"Okay, but I'm bringing Tom with me."

"Tom is already at the bakery helping with their sale, dear."

Joy clicked her tongue. "Darn, I knew that."

"So get going."

Joy gestured toward her striped and spangled elf outfit. "Like this?"

"Joy, it's the holiday season. Besides, where you're going? Do you think anyone will look twice at you?"

Joy had to agree to that statement. This store was known for its shoppers wearing anything and everything, or nearly nothing. In fact, there were whole websites dedicated to posting pictures of the hapless customers, their identities artfully disguised with blurs and black boxes.

"Let's just hope I don't end up on there," she grumbled.

Joy caught a glimpse of herself in the big mirror set above the overstuffed couch. The long-sleeved green leotard was one thing, with its scooped and fake-fur trimmed collar. The matching puffy tulle skirt all but covered in jingle bells was another. She wasn't even going to look at her red-and-white striped tights or green shoes right now. True, she wasn't wearing the hat or pointy ears right now. She'd pulled her hair up in a high ponytail and the bright red bow on top gave her the look of a peppermint cheerleader.

Bells punctuating her every step, she went out to the parking lot and got into her Jeep. It took a few cranks to start, and she made a mental note to have Claire Chapman's dad Callie take a look at it.

Heading out of Cypress, she maneuvered around the ladders and busy volunteers decking out the square. Her favorite radio station had been playing holiday songs almost since Halloween, so she bopped along to Johnny Mathis. She might have given her mother a hard time yesterday, but Black Friday did start the holiday season for Joy.

As she passed the coffee shop, she spied Lettie in her usual spot beneath the naked branches of a crepe myrtle tree. The older woman was a fixture on the square, and today she wore a thick nubby sweater over her usual flowered smock. Joy waved and Lettie lifted her cardboard coffee cup in salute.

A Peanuts jazzy number played on the radio as she pulled into the shopping center parking lot. St. Cloud was about fifteen minutes to the west from Cypress Corners. As she'd fully expected, the lot was packed. After parking in a space that felt like it was a hundred miles away from the entrance, she grabbed an abandoned cart and made her way into the throng.

By the time she'd loaded up on lights and candy canes, paid and was out the door, she had to face the fact that her mother had actually been wrong for once. There wasn't one person, aside from those fighting for deals on flat screen TVs, who didn't remark on her outfit. Lucky for her, and for them, she was full of the holiday spirit and simply smiled.

After loading her car, she passed off the shopping cart to a grateful shopper and turned the ignition. It sputtered like it had earlier, but started at last. Singing along to Brenda Lee, she rocked her way back toward Cypress.

Once she drove out of St. Cloud itself, the landscape changed. It was subtle, but almost before a driver realized it they were in the country. This was what some people referred to as Old Florida. Scrubby brush, tall cypress trees and acres and acres of rolling land. Cattle country, believe it or not. She sure hadn't when she'd first moved her.

The fifteen minute stretch between the city and Cypress Corners was an easy ride, with only one blinking light. Just as she passed that hapless intersection, her Jeep gave a lurch.

"What the…" The car didn't answer, but just bucked again.

It started to slow down and she pressed her foot harder to the gas pedal. Nothing. Glancing in her rearview mirror, she saw that there was no one behind her. That made sense. Everyone in the world was at the big store shopping for Black Friday deals. There was no one in front of her, either.

"Darn it."

She jerked the wheel just in time for the vehicle to coast to a slow stop on the sandy shoulder of the road. Cranking the key in the ignition did nothing but tick the engine off, so she turned it completely off.

A glance at her phone showed her what she should have figured out ahead of time. There was always spotty service on this road, and she was lucky enough to stall in a big empty spot.

She stepped out of the car, resisting the urge to slam the heck out of the door. It was chilly today, and breezy. Her frilly skirt blew up around her butt, its bells jangling merrily.

"This is just great," she grumbled.

She had to walk to where she could pick up a cell signal. She couldn't just sit here with fifteen hundred candy canes, could she? Her Jeep had conked out just about halfway between the city and Cypress, so she figured she might as well head for home. She grabbed her purse and locked the Jeep, and blew out a resigned breath.

Then she saw something on the horizon, coming from the direction of St. Cloud. She squinted, trying to make out the shape that was getting bigger as it made its way closer.

"Is that a horse?" she murmured, shielding her eyes from the afternoon glare.

It was! More than that? It was a horse and rider, and headed straight for her. But it was the identity of the rider that blew her mind.

It was Zach Harris. Relief spread through her, along with a healthy dose of surprise and heat. Old Scrooge himself.

***

Zach slowed his horse as he approached the stranded car. There was a sexy little elf standing beside a dusty Jeep that had obviously seen better days. It was a strange sight, for sure. When she waved a hand, he decided it wasn't so strange after all. Nope. It made perfect sense that his brunette was here on the side of the road dressed like a Christmas elf. For a second he wondered if he'd cracked his head back at the ranch and was still stretched out in a stupor on the kitchen floor.

"Hey there, Jingles," he said as he reined in the horse.

"Jingles?" She huffed and crossed her arms, showing off the impressive cleavage trimmed by white fur at the top of her costume. "Hey there, yourself."

His lips twitched and he shook his head. "Do I even want to know?"

"I'm not sure." She cocked her head to the side, her eyes sparkling. "I'm on my way home from St. Cloud with one hundred and fifty boxes of candy canes. Just a normal day."

He barked out a laugh. His horse looked back at him, apparently surprised to hear him make the sound. He sure as hell was. He couldn't remember the last time he'd laughed.

"Jeep stopped?"

She arched a brow and pursed her lips. How could a woman be sexy and adorable at the same time? Her legs looked really long in those striped tights, too.

He dismounted and walked toward her, holding the horse's reins. "All right, that's obvious. What happened?"

"I don't know." She uncrossed her arms and threw her car an exasperated look. "It gave me a couple of fits while I was starting it, and then halfway home it just slowed down."

Zach nodded. "Sounds like it might be the gas filter. Or maybe the battery."

"The battery?" She stepped away from the horse, her gaze cautious now. "I don't think Trigger here can jump it for me."

He felt like grinning now. "Nope. I'll take you home, Jingles."

"On that?"

"On *him*." He leveled a look at her. "He has a name."

"Okay, on Trigger?"

"It's Chestnut, and yes."

"I told you yesterday, I don't ride."

He grabbed her around her waist and hoisted her up on the horse. "Today, you do."

She looked terrified, her pretty brown eyes opened wide, so he didn't tease her. He mounted behind her and urged the horse into a gentle trot.

She sighed, soft and low. "So you're my knight in shining armor?"

"Never been called that before, but sure."

They rode on for a few minutes, her lush body stiff in front of him. Forcing his gaze away from the view down the front of her, he kept the horse to an easy pace.

"Aren't you going to ask me about my clothes?" she asked.

"I don't know what you're into, Jingles. Not my place."

She gave his hand a playful slap. "Never mind. We're in full holiday mode at the inn."

"Hence the candy canes?"

"And twinkly lights."

He nodded and caught a bit of her minty hot scent. "Of course."

"You just ride around on a horse all the time?"

"Not all the time, no. Billy asked me to ride over and help pace out the size of the new stables. We got to talking about them yesterday, as a matter of fact."

"Right. I think they're going to go to the east of Billy and Shannon's place."

"You know a lot about what's going on, then?"

"I'm a Cypress Corners girl, Zach. I've been here since the beginning."

"Which isn't as far back as it looks, right?"

She glanced at him over her shoulder. "Was there a compliment in there?"

"Jingles, if I was going to compliment you it would be on these pretty peppermint legs."

She shook her head, sending more of her scent up into his nose from that perky ponytail of hers as she faced forward again. "Why didn't you take the horse in a trailer?"

"Because Chestnut needed a ride and so did I."

She turned her head to regard him over one shoulder, and he managed to swallow the naughty things he wanted to add. She fit really good against him, slender and curved, and he hadn't been kidding about her legs. He had a really nice view of them at the moment.

"Thank you," she said softly.

"No problem."

They reached Cypress Corners within a half an hour, and by the time he saw the white ranch fencing he was really started to regret hauling her to sit up in front of him. She was soft. Warm. And he was getting really uncomfortable in his jeans.

As they rode into Cypress, he could see that the decorating was nearly finished. With surprising thoroughness, too. He doubted there was a tree limb or lamppost left bare of ribbons and greenery. In fact, there were still people on ladders hanging ornaments and strings of lights as they rode up to the strip of shops on the square.

"Jeez, they did all of this today?"

"It's not their first rodeo." She laughed, amused at her turn of phrase. "Sorry. Couldn't resist."

"Chestnut takes no offense. It's not his first, either."

"Do you make a habit of rescuing damsels in distress on your, well, brown steed?"

"He's not brown, he's chestnut. But not a habit. No."

"Chestnuts roasting on an open fire…" She sang with a voice as clear as a bell, and then stopped and gave a shrug. "Sorry. It's a hazard of the season."

"Christmas carols and dressing like an elf? This is normal for you?"

"The singing, sadly yes. At this time of the year, anyway. The elf costume? This is a new torture my mother came up with for the photo op."

"What's the photo op?"

"At the inn." She blew out a breath. "She wants to make certain that everyone has their holiday card picture taken at the inn."

"Are you in the picture?"

That brow arched again as she glanced over at him. "Uh, no."

"Just asking." He smiled then. "Seems to me that any guy would be willing to sit for a picture with a sexy elf girl next to him."

Heat flared in her eyes and he tried to remember what he'd just said to her. If he could get that kind of reaction from a silly line, what would happen if he ever figured out how to really turn on the Harris charm? The good Lord knew he hadn't gotten much of what Chase and Billy seemed to have in abundance.

"Where to, Jingles?"

She rolled her eyes. "That's not going to stop, is it?"

"Not any time soon, I bet." He nudged her a little. "A guy gets his jollies where he can."

Now she turned almost fully in the saddle. "Oh my gosh, did you just make a joke?"

"I think I might have."

"So no Christmas spirit, clearly. But at least a little sense of humor?"

He shrugged in answer. And she smiled.

"Where to?" he asked as they stopped in front of the coffee shop.

"I guess here is okay. I have to get somebody to go get the Jeep. And the candy canes and lights."

He dismounted and helped her down. He sure liked having his hands on her, and wondered if she'd laugh again or slap him if he pulled her in a little closer.

"Well, hello there Joy!" an older woman called from one of the tables in the courtyard of the coffee shop.

"Hi, Lettie."

"And who is that handsome cowboy with you?" the lady asked in a voice dripping with southern flavor.

Zach stepped back to nod to the woman. "Zach Harris, ma'am."

"Charlotte Fairfax, but you can call me Lettie like everyone does."

"Thank you, ma'am."

Bright blue eyes under a silvery fringe of bangs widened and then the lady grinned. "Southern gentleman, are you?"

"I'm afraid so," he answered. "Born and raised in St. Cloud."

She gave a slow nod, resting her folded arms on the wrought iron table. "Seems to me you look awfully familiar."

"You probably know his brother, Lettie," Joy said. "Chase. Or his cousin Billy."

The woman's eyes narrowed and Zach felt like she could see inside of him. "Oh my, yes. But there's something else there." She made a show of fanning herself with what looked like a seed catalog. "Still, those Harris boys sure are something to look at. And you, Zach Harris, are no disappointment in that department."

He heard Joy chuckle under her breath and managed to keep his own expression even.

"Her car broke down."

"Is that why you're squiring our dear Joy around the town square on that magnificent animal?"

"Yes, ma'am."

"Then you need to come in here and have yourself a cup of hot cocoa, Joy. Dip a peppermint stick in it the way I know you like it."

Zach filed that nugget of information away for later. The girl like chocolate and peppermint, which explained why she always smelled so damn good.

"Let me text my brother, Joy." He pulled his cell out of his pocket. "I'm sure he and I can run out to your Jeep and at least get it back here for you."

"Thanks, Zach."

It seemed like she wanted to say more, and he stared at her lips for a long minute. Would those lips taste sweet, too? He just bet they would. Another flash of heat cut through the chilled air around them.

"Call your mother before she starts to worry about you, dear," Lettie said.

Zach hadn't thought of that, but then he'd never had anyone at home waiting for him. Or worrying about him. He shoved that thought aside and focused on getting Joy's car back. He'd ponder the way she had him all twisted up later. A smile teased his lips. Peppermint twisted.

He texted Chase that he was coming and then told her he'd be back with Chase. He dipped his head in Lettie's direction and mounted Chestnut for the short ride out toward the east side of the property.

As the road gradually shifted from pavement to sandy soil, he thought about Joy. There was something about this girl. Something he'd never encountered before. She was full of the Christmas spirit and a whole lot of spunk, and to his surprise he'd been tempted to kiss her right there on the street. Just grab her and kiss her until every bell on that sinful little skirt rang loud enough for everybody to hear.

He figured that Lettie woman didn't miss a thing, though. He'd caught the speculation in her gaze for sure, and he wouldn't do anything to rile Joy up. Not in public anyway. In private, though?

If he ever got her all to himself he'd enjoy riling her all kinds of up.

Chapter 4

"I think you'll be happy." The realtor, a woman with curly brown hair with a whole lot of cleavage showing in the deep V of her blouse, leaned forward with a smile. "Who wouldn't be?"

Not him. Zach just nodded. "Thanks for all your hard work."

She waved a hand and rested her folded arms on the scarred wooden table that had seen lots of roughhousing and little domesticity when he and his brother and cousin were growing up.

"I'm making a very nice commission on this sale, Mr. Harris. And the buyers are paying a premium to take possession before Christmas."

He figured that was true. And by the dollar signs he could see in her eyes? She was pretty happy herself.

"So that's it, then," he said.

She blinked at him. "All done but for scheduling the closing."

Zach stood and shook her hand. He could see something else in her eyes now. A warmth, sure. But maybe an invitation, too. It was something that he might have considered if he wasn't doing business with her. Something he might have thought could

48

be a pretty good way to pass a couple of hours, if he hadn't spent the past few days thinking about a different brunette. One who had him all peppermint-twisted.

He just smiled at her.

"I'll be in touch." She gathered the papers and Zach showed her out. Sitting back down at the table alone, he pulled out his phone. Tapping on Chase's name, he settled back against the hard bench seat.

"Hey, bro," Chase answered.

"It's done," was all Zach could get past the lump in his throat.

Chase was quiet for a long minute, then he gave a low whistle. "I can't believe it."

"Believe it." Zach closed his eyes. "The Harris ranch won't belong to a Harris in a few weeks. Probably by Christmas. We're getting paid a nice chunk of change to make that happen."

"No shit? Damn."

Exactly. Zach nodded, though his brother couldn't see it.

"Why don't you come out to Cypress and celebrate? I know Carrie would like to see your ugly mug. Not to mention Caitlyn."

"You're still staying out at Billy's place. I don't want to

intrude."

"Yeah, but at least Carrie and I will have our own place soon."

"In Cypress?"

"Where else?"

Zach was quiet for a minute. Now his brother was putting down roots there like Billy? Zach wanted to go to Cypress, but he was almost afraid of what would happen if he ran into Joy. He could still picture her as she'd been on Friday, the three days since passing in a whirlwind of showings and offers to buy the ranch. God, she was adorable. And hot. And sweet, like a peppermint stick. Damn, she'd smelled good up close. And felt good pressed against him, too.

She was all about the holiday, though. And she had ties he couldn't begin to understand there in Stepford. He was better off just hooking up with some random woman now and then, like he'd done for years now. He'd never had a girlfriend in high school. Never had a sweetheart or even a girl he thought about when she wasn't right in front of him. He was thirty-one years old now, and he didn't even know how to date. And Joy Rollins was a woman a man dated. Took to dinner. Romanced. He didn't know a lick about romance.

"Bro?"

Chase's voice brought him back to their conversation.

"I'll think about it."

"Look, get the hell off of the ranch and come out to Cypress. You don't have to come to Billy and Shannon's. We can meet at the Town Tavern."

Zach glanced at the time on his phone and put it back to his ear. "What time?"

He could almost hear Chase smiling over the connection. "Seven okay? Becky's coming over to watch Caitlyn after her bed time."

"Seven's good."

The brothers disconnected the call and Zach sat back and looked around the kitchen. He tried to picture anything warm and fuzzy from his childhood there in the functional if spartan room. Yeah, he and his brother and cousin had done their homework at this table. He had mixed feelings about his mother's teaching him to read there, though. He'd known he was a burden, and as a kid he'd wondered if having a son who needed extra attention had helped push her out the door.

Family dinners weren't quite what he figured most kids' were, either. Theirs had always been a bachelor household.

Wild Harry Harris never cooked more than steak and potatoes for the boys growing up, although the women from St. Cloud of marrying age had brought over casseroles, cakes and just about anything else that might have tempted the old man to consider remarrying. Nothing would touch Harry, though. Zach wasn't sure if he was brokenhearted over his wife's leaving or if he was just done with women in general. None of the women, although very nice and motherly for the most part, had made him forego his solitude. Their father had been like a widower, and never mentioned their absent mother.

Billy's parents were mentioned, though. They were killed in a one-car accident on a rain-slick road, and mourned openly by Harry when he had too much to drink. This wasn't often, despite his nickname. Losing his younger brother had affected him in his heart, it seemed. Losing his wife? That seemed to close up his heart but good.

Zach scrubbed a hand over his face, feeling a dampness around his eyes he chose to ignore. He wasn't even sure why he would miss the ranch. The buyers wanted all of the stock too, and Zach and Chase had agreed that made sense. So except for a few of their favorite horses, all of the animals would belong to the new family moving into the ranch house. He felt strange about selling everything. Not like he was losing a part of himself. No. In truth, he felt disconnected.

Zach had worked through the words of the offer contract as best he could, secretly grateful that the realtor seemed to delight in pointing out every little detail. That was a good thing, because details in writing? Not Zach's strong suit.

He'd had reading difficulties in school, but his mother's occasional help and the help of a few caring teachers, he'd learned how to cope by the time he was in high school. How to cheat, so to speak. How to get along. Numbers he could handle. And teaching himself to get along had served him pretty well, considering that his job was taking care of the ranch and the animals and seeing to the books. Chase was a word guy, but there wasn't much required in that department.

Zach stood, clutching the edge of the table for a second. He was headed out to Cypress. To hang out with family. To celebrate the fact that the family ranch would no longer belong to the family.

He knew it was the right thing. In his head. Hell, even in his heart. There were no emotional ties to this place for any of them. Not on Chase or Billy's side and certainly not on Zach's.

"Now I just have to figure out what the hell I'm going to

do with the rest of my life."

By the time he arrived at Cypress, he was resigned to celebrating. So to speak. His brother, and maybe even Billy, would be there and that would be nice. He'd seen how close Chase and Billy had become over the past year, and he figured he should try to grab on to some of that for himself. He wouldn't think about the fact that he had no attachments of any kind now. Not to the land. Not to his family's legacy. He had a whole boatload of cash though, or would before the New Year.

The Town Tavern at Cypress didn't look at all like he'd expected. It was cozy with dark wood paneling and green-shaded lamps. There was a murmur of conversation coming from what he guessed was the bar area, and he walked up to the hostess stand. The girl behind the stand turned and he was face to face with the woman he couldn't stop thinking about for the last three days.

"Zach." She gave him that slow smile that made him think about sipping peppermint hot chocolate after a chilly morning out with the herd.

He couldn't explain it, but it made him feel like hunkering down and not coming up until Groundhog Day.

***

"What are you doing here?" Joy asked.

His eyes flicked over her and she stifled a tingle. "Celebrating, Jingles."

"Celebrating what?"

He opened his mouth to answer, but a big hand clapped him on the shoulder.

"Big brother here just sold the ranch!" Chase said with a grin.

Zach smiled and nodded. Joy looked at him closely, her brows drawn together. "Is that like buying the farm?"

Chase laughed out loud but Zach just shook his head.

"We're here to drink, Joy," Carrie said. "The baby's asleep and my hubby and I are going to toast our financial upswing."

Joy looked at Zach again, and then nodded with a smile. "Then congratulations. I take it you'll be buying a place here now, Chase?"

"Hope to," Chase said. "Can't risk overstaying our welcome over at Billy and Shannon's, now can we?"

Zach said nothing, his brow slightly furrowed. What was that about? She got the sense that he had some seriously mixed feelings about selling the ranch.

Joy led them to one of the tables set near the fire crackling behind the glass and brass doors of the hearth. The atmosphere was very welcoming in the tavern, and maybe Zach could sort through his feelings over a couple of cold ones with his brother. Wasn't that was guys did? She had no real clue. She and Tom didn't exactly pal around.

"Bar food is listed on the table," Joy told them. "Flag me down and I'll take your order for drinks, too."

"Why are you working here tonight?" Carrie asked.

Joy shrugged. "I work wherever and whenever I can, Carrie."

"Aren't you teaching?"

She shook her head, her ponytail swinging. "If only. No, it seems most teachers used up their vacation days way before the end of the semester. No substitute openings have been posted for a couple of weeks now."

She hurried off to the hostess stand again, but she saw that Zach followed her with his gaze. The place did a good business, even on a Monday. She was grateful for that at the moment, because ever since he'd walked in she'd just wanted to stare at him. His thick leather jacket was now on the back of his chair and his broad shoulders were wrapped in one of those flannel-chambray shirts in a shade of blue that made his eyes appear dark green. The sleeves were pushed up on his arms, he had very nice arms, and he leaned forward.

She filled three glasses with water and took a breath before heading back over to their table.

"What about getting a big pizza pie, bro?" Chase asked as she set them down.

"Ooh, with pineapple?" Carrie asked.

Both Harris brother's groaned.

"We're having meat, honey," Chase said. "Zach here would faint if we had fruit on a pizza."

Zach shrugged. "Order whatever you want on it. I'm getting a burger."

Joy wrinkled her nose. She wasn't a fan of pineapple on a pizza herself. She gave Zach a slow nod in mock-seriousness. "Eating a burger, Zach? Are you already missing those cows of yours?"

"Cattle, Jingles. And don't tell me you're one of those people who doesn't eat meat."

His eyes sparkled and she was seized with the urge to give as good as she got. He was quicker than she'd thought at first last week. Still waters, and all of that. She'd had him right on that count.

"Don't assume things, Cowboy."

Chase chuckled and Zach stared at her as she straightened.

"What are you guys drinking?" Joy asked.

"Two bottles of Bud for me and my brother," Chase said. "Baby, what do you want?"

Carrie's forehead wrinkled for a second. "Oh, I better just stick with water. I'm still breastfeeding."

Zach's cheeks flushed red at that disclosure. He picked up his water and took a good long drink.

"Earth to Zach," Carrie said, waving a hand.

He blinked and focused on his sister-in-law. "Yeah?"

"Sorry about the TMI," she said with a laugh.

He gave her a short nod of thanks. Joy hid her smile. Yeah, it was too-much-information. It was funny to see such a big strong guy blush, though. She grabbed the bottles of beer and went back to their table.

"Do you know when the closing will be?" Carrie asked.

"The realtor said it should be all said and done by Christmas," Zach said.

"Wow," Carrie said. "That's fast."

"According to the realtor, they're very motivated. I'll send you the papers Chase, but I told you they might want it all, right?

They do want it all. Lock, stock and barrel."

"Where will you go?" Joy asked.

Zach's brows rose and his lips parted. "I don't know."

Chase and Carrie exchanged a look Joy couldn't decipher.

"You can stay at the inn," Joy said, and then she bit her lower lip. "We have the room, I think."

Carrie clasped her hands. "Oh Zach, that would be fun! It's all done up for Christmas, you know."

That apparently made Zach smile a little in Joy's direction. "Yep. I know."

Joy snorted a little laugh. "So, meat on your pizza?"

Chase nodded and Carrie grumbled a little. "Sausage, please."

"Burger for Zach," Joy said. "Let me guess. Rare?"

"Medium rare will do, thanks," Zach said.

He sipped his beer and Chase and Carrie started to talk about the different villages in Cypress. Joy waited on a couple of other tables, her mind working. She idly wondered where Chase and his little family would settle.

"Where do you want to look, baby?" Chase asked Carrie as Joy brought their meals to the table. "I bet we can head over to the Sales Center tomorrow and Jessie will be happy to show us what she has."

"Jessie's one of the top salespeople in Cypress," Joy said.

"That's what Billy says, too," Carrie said with a smile.

"He must know what he's talking about, since he's married to Jessie's sister," Chase said.

"Where do you think we should look, Joy?" Carrie asked.

"Well, there are some gorgeous homes set near the lakeshore," Joy said. "Although most of the houses here are pretty, even the smaller ones in the other villages."

She left them to their meals and by the time she put in the orders for the large party in the big room in the back, Zach was alone. His expression was unreadable, and he was peeling the label off the neck of his empty beer bottle. Like when she'd first seen him on Thanksgiving, she made the decision to put a smile on that handsome face.

After a quick stop at the bar to grab him another beer, she placed it on his table and crossed her arms.

"All by your lonesome, Cowboy?"

He glanced up and as she watched those sculpted lips of his curved up at one corner. "Not anymore."

Chapter 5

Zach's answer startled a laugh out of her.

"Smooth, Zach." She opened her mouth to say something more, but just then a customer at another table called out for her.

She all but flew her way over there, smiling and nodding to the elderly couple. He'd been watching her bustle around the place like she ran on batteries. Even while Chase and Carrie had talked, his attention kept straying to Joy. That was no loss, as far as he was concerned. Figuring out some of their marriage-speak had been beyond him.

It was a lot like reading a book for class and having to come up with the motivation of a character or some sort of shit like that. He was never good at reading of any kind, and he sure as hell couldn't gauge their expressions. Not when they were traded between married people who seemed to speak their own language.

Joy made a very nice picture tonight. Hot and sweet, and easy on the eyes. She wore a pair of dark jeans and a long-sleeve shirt the color of a thick rare steak. It was a great color on her, but he figured it would be just as pretty off of her.

After taking care of whatever those older folks needed, she slid into one of the vacant chairs at his table and leaned her elbows on the table. "So are you going to move into the inn?"

"I don't think so."

"You'd be close to family, Zach. For Christmas."

"Yep. That's what Carrie said."

"So they want you around."

"I might not know my sister-in-law very well, but she and Chase seem pretty damn perfect for each other, Joy. And with their little carrottop added to the mix? I wouldn't make a difference in their holiday either way."

Her eyes shimmered. "The holidays are made for family, Zach."

"I don't do holidays," he said. "Sorry."

Now she winked at him. "Seems to me you got into the spirit just this past Friday."

Zach's lower half reacted a little at the memory of the sexy elf nestled so close to him on top of Chestnut.

"It was pretty hard to ignore you, Jingles."

"Move to the inn, Zach." She placed a hand over his. Her fingers were warm and her skin was soft. "At least for a little while."

He narrowed his eyes on her. "Until when?"

Her pretty brown eyes twinkled merrily at him. "Until

Christmas."

He gave a slow shake of his head. "Do you think I'll be caught by the spirit by then?"

"Maybe. I'm not giving up on you yet."

"It's just wishful thinking, Joy. I'll get through the holidays and then find a new place to live. For good."

Her brows knit and she withdrew her hand. The loss of contact left him a little cold.

"Get through?" Her eyes opened wide. "Zach, the holidays are when anything can happen. Especially in Cypress Corners."

"Anything?" He barked out a laugh. "You've had one too many candy canes."

She looked thoughtful, and more than a little adorable. Her nose wrinkled and her lips pursed. Then she nodded. "Give Cypress a chance. I am."

"You're giving it a chance? Hell, Joy. You are Cypress."

A flash of something, maybe sadness, crossed her face. It was gone in an instant and she beamed a smile. The full-watt grin sent all kinds of thoughts through his head, and not a one of them had to do with Christmas.

"Let me show you how to do Christmas, Zach."

"No. No way. I don't need a holly jolly tour guide,

thanks."

"Holly jolly?" She laughed lightly. "You're not as lost a cause as you think, Cowboy."

"Miss?" The gray-haired woman from the table across the way waved a hand. "Excuse me, miss?"

Joy stood. "Be right there, ma'am." She turned and studied Zach for a beat. "Think about it?"

Zach just picked up the beer she'd brought him and took a drink.

What if he did decide to move to Cypress? He could see her every day. He might not be boyfriend material, but he knew he was a pretty good time. He might even be good enough for her to waste a little of her time with him. Although from what he already knew about her? She didn't have a lot of it to spare.

He only sipped at the beer she'd brought him, his mind wrapped around the seemingly endless future laid out in front of him. Should he stay in St. Cloud? The ranch was on the outskirts, and he didn't really care for buying one of the older homes set out in the city proper. The grid of streets all bore state names, and the houses were almost all built over forty years ago.

Carrie and Chase had continued to discuss the different places in Cypress where they could set down roots even after their pizza was gone. They had their little carrottop, after all. There was a lot at stake for them. As for Zach? He could just as soon pick any place and be happy. Okay, not exactly happy. Content. That might be all he could hope for.

He watched Joy for a long minute, imagining what it might be like to take her up on her challenge. And that's what it sure felt like to him. A challenge to give Christmas a chance, of all things.

She came to his table again, and stood with one hip cocked to the side. "Well?"

"You got a deal."

She blinked long lashes at him, her brows drawn together. "What?"

"I'll move into the inn, Joy. If you're sure there's room."

She brightened, her hands clasped. The delight on her face made agreeing worthwhile.

"Oh! I was just coming by to see if you needed anything else, but yay! You'll love it."

He arched a brow and she snorted a little laugh as she sat down across from him again.

"Okay, maybe not love it. But you won't hate it. I promise."

"If you say so."

A spark of something came into her eyes and she tilted her head. "How do you feel about cinnamon?"

He arched a brow again and she blushed a little.

"The inn is famous for its cinnamon rolls," she rushed out.

"Cinnamon is okay, I guess." He leaned toward her, breathing deeply of her scent. "But I think I prefer peppermint."

Their lips were just inches apart, and he longed for a taste of hers. Her breathing hitched and he felt a shiver of want. He looked deep into her eyes, letting her see what he was feeling. Her pupils dilated and she licked her lips.

Another customer called out to her and the moment was lost. He sat back and finished his beer. Tonight he might have missed his chance. He would be living at the inn, though. Under the same roof with her.

If he ever got close to kissing her again? He'd make sure there was nobody around to stop him from giving in to what they both wanted.

***

Joy woke at seven on Tuesday morning, more of less ready for her shift at the inn. Her mother ran a tight ship, after all. Joy had finished up at the tavern just after eleven last night, and

Zach had hung around until closing time. She'd gotten the feeling that he'd wanted to talk some more. That was weird, since he didn't seem like a chatty kind of guy. Her? She was a chatterbox and always had been.

She donned a more-subdued version of the elf girl costume she'd worn on Black Friday, sparkly green-striped leggings and an almost-ugly holiday sweater. Today's was red and featured a grinning reindeer with a noticeably red nose. That lit up.

"Way to go, Mom."

Joy smiled to herself. The sweater was soft and comfy and the leggings made her legs look long, so she wasn't going to grouse too much about it. She wouldn't let her mother know she was okay with it, though. Goodness knew what Karen Rollins would come up with for tomorrow.

The bells sewn onto her sweater tinkled as she pranced down the stairs. Ballet flats made her steps almost silent, and she snuck into the dining room as best she could wearing an arsenal of jingle bells. It was full of guests, she wasn't surprised to find. Thanksgiving might be over and Christmas weeks away, but there were plenty of people eager for a touch of holiday spirit in sunny Florida.

"Here's our girl!" her mother called.

Joy skidded to a stop in the doorway, quickly eyeing the tray of cinnamon rolls. There were only a few left. Darn. They were one of favorite things about living at the inn, and it looked like she might have missed out on them today.

"Good morning," Joy said with a smile.

The older couple, the same people she'd waited on last night at the tavern, smiled in return.

"Oh, you look adorable!" the woman said.

The guest was dressed smartly in a velvet tunic and pressed jeans tucked into low boots. That was the thing about Florida seniors, in their part of Florida at least. They liked to dress and weren't afraid to push the envelope past velvet track suits.

"Thank you," Joy said. "I didn't know you were staying here."

"Just moved in," her husband said. "Came down here from Orlando to check out the Active Adult community."

"That's becoming very popular," her mother said. "Joy, don't you know folks who live over there?"

Joy had to hand it to her mother. The woman knew how to sell Cypress and she'd never set foot in the Sales Center.

"Yes, my friend Bree's future mother-in-law is moving in there soon."

The woman clasped her hands. "Oh! How exciting."

"I guess," the husband said. "I'm just thinking about that golf course being dangerously close by." He dropped a wink in Joy's direction. "I know my weaknesses."

Joy nodded. "There's lots to do there. Have you taken a tour?"

"Yes, but today we're headed to the Cypress Institute."

"My other daughter, Becky, works there," Joy's mother said. "She'll help set you up with anything you like."

They nodded and Joy took the lull in conversation as an opportunity to hurry to the sideboard for what looked like the last cinnamon roll. After glancing over her shoulder to make sure her mother wasn't watching, she reached out for the pastry. And found her hand grasped by a much larger one.

"Oh no you don't, Jingles."

Her heart dropped to her belly and she whipped her head around to find Zach Harris standing there. "What are you doing?" She swallowed, tugging her hand back from his. "Here. I mean, what are you doing here?"

He crossed his arms over his impressive chest. He wore soft-looking tan corduroys on his long legs and his thin cable-knit sweater was a Florida-winter version of a fisherman's and did really nice things to those shoulders of his. Sneakers instead of cowboy boots today, so he mustn't have ridden to Cypress on his horse.

"Did you or did you not tell me there was room at the inn?" His eyes sparkled. "Or do I have to stay in the stable?"

She blinked, then laughed out loud. "Another Christmas joke, Zach? You sure are learning."

He shrugged. "I've been told that Christmas is something to savor, or something like that."

She searched her mind for what she'd actually said to him last night, but couldn't seem to think with his gorgeous blue eyes staring into hers. Instead, she watched as he snagged the cinnamon roll. They were tucked into little brown sleeves just ready for takeout.

"Oh, did you want this?" he teased.

Placing her hands on her hips, she tilted her head. "You're the guest."

He slid the roll onto a plate. "How about we split it?"

"Joy, what are you doing?" her mother said as she sailed over to where they stood.

"Nothing at all, Mom." Joy kept her eye on Zach. "Just wishing our new guest here a good morning."

"How did you find your breakfast, Mr. Harris?"

"Delicious, Mrs. Rollins. Your daughter told me all about the cinnamon rolls but she didn't say anything about the coffee."

Her mother giggled, actually giggled, and waved a hand. "Oh, we have nothing on the coffee shop in town in that department but thank you for saying so."

Zack dipped his head, raising his dish in Joy's direction. "I was just going to split this with your daughter."

"Joy wouldn't think of depriving you of whatever you want, Mr. Harris."

Joy flushed hot as his gaze ran over her. Her tilted a smile in her direction and then turned to face her mother again.

"Is that so?" At her mother's nod, he smiled. "Then I want a little company for breakfast. Unless you need her for something?"

Her mother shook her head, her red-and-gray curls bouncing around her face. She was in Mrs. Claus mode again today, but to Joy that was just the new normal.

"Joy will show you to your room when you're ready. Mr. Harris is in room number seven, Joy."

With that, her mother left Joy alone with a guy more tempting than the icing on those lauded cinnamon rolls. She sat down at a little table set near the French doors leading to the terrace and waited for him to join her.

"Coffee?" he asked her.

"Gallons," she said. "Cream and sweetener, please."

He chuckled and brought her a perfectly stirred café au lait cup and two yellow packets of sweetener before sitting across from her. He cut the roll in half and put her share on another plate. "So what do you do here at the inn?"

She leveled a look at him. "Anything and everything."

"That's what you always say."

"Always?"

"Every time I've asked you what you do, anyway."

"I'll admit I'm a little scattered."

He took a bite of his roll, his eyes going wide before closing in obvious pleasure. "Oh my God," he mumbled around a mouthful of icing and spice.

Joy took a small bite of hers. "I know. My mother is pretty proud of these babies."

He finished his in another big bite and wiped his mouth on a napkin. "She should be. Do you bake these?"

"I know how, but I don't usually make them. These are my mother's thing."

"You bake, though?"

"Why? Are you hungry?"

He stared at her for a beat. "Not touching that one, Jingles. I like the outfit today, by the way."

His eyes were fastened to the blinking lights on her chest.

"Big surprise," she said.

He smiled again. Man, he had a nice smile.

"Are you working tonight?"

"Here?"

"Anywhere, Joy. Are you working anywhere tonight."

"I actually have the night off. I was going to…" She cut herself off. She knew what she wanted to do tonight but suspected it would be yet another exercise in futility. No matter the free time she managed to carve out for herself, she just couldn't find any inspiration to create anything at all.

"What were you going to do?"

"Never mind."

He looked like he was going to ask her something more, but he just gave another shrug. "Then maybe you might want to come out with me? Hit the End Zone and shoot a couple of games of pool."

That brightened her spirits more than the twinkling lights

on her sweater. "That sounds fun."

He nodded. "Good. I have to head into town to see to a few things later. Maybe you could come with me and then we can eat on the way back."

She bit her lip. "I guess so."

"When are you finished here?"

"My mother usually cuts me loose around three."

He nodded again, wiping his mouth with a napkin. "That would be great. I'm thinking of letting Chase and Carrie take a look at the furniture at the ranch. See if they want anything."

She wasn't sure where this was going. "Are they coming with us?"

"No. I wanted your opinion on what I should keep for myself."

She held up her hands. "Zach, I have no idea what you like."

Those pretty eyes of his sparkled. "Don't you?"

Whoa, was it hot in here or was it him?

He shot her a quick smile and came to his feet. "I'm going to head out to Billy's place in a little while. How about the nickel tour?"

"For you?" She stood, barely reaching his broad shoulders

in her ballet flats. "It won't cost you a thing."

"Then I'll owe you, Jingles."

She couldn't say anything as she led the way out of the dining room, but his hand on her arm stilled her. "What?"

He raised his eyes skyward, and she saw they were under a sprig of mistletoe. No big surprise there, since her mother had stuck the stuff on just about every doorway. She brought her gaze back to him and saw his lips were curved again. She caught his scent, that delicious smell of fresh hot outdoors that she'd noticed clung to him.

"Zach." She swallowed thickly, her pulse racing. "What are you doing?"

"Getting into the Christmas spirit," he drawled.

Then his lips settled over hers.

Chapter 6

Zach felt a zing sweeter than peppermint as he tasted Joy's delectable lips. Her mouth was soft. Wet. And he couldn't resist sweeping his tongue across her lips before pulling back.

She stared up at him for a beat and then she sighed. That was a pretty nice sound.

"Mistletoe, Jingles."

She gave a shaky laugh and stepped back, her gaze searching the dining room. He did likewise, but didn't find anything to worry about in his own sweep of the room. Joy's mother was still engaged with a few of the guests over at the coffee station, so he figured she'd missed his momentary lapse in judgment. Damn, but he liked kissing Joy.

"Your room," Joy said, her insistence sounding a little weak.

"Lead on," he said with a tilt of his chin.

Her candy-striped legs took to the curved staircase and he watched as he followed behind. She seemed to shift into hostess mode with every step.

"The Cypress Inn is three stories tall, and sits on a rise not far from the main lakeshore."

He just nodded, knowing no answer was needed. The bed

and breakfast was designed well, and situated in a near-perfect setting. He'd checked out the huge wraparound porch as he'd approached that morning, and noticed that there were wide balconies off of several of the guest rooms. He'd asked Mrs. Rollins for one of those rooms. Why the hell not? He could sure use a view out toward the lake. It was so different than the dusty brown view out of just about every window of the ranch house.

"Here's your room," she said, stopping at a door on the second floor. "Number seven."

"Lucky me," he said.

That made her smile appear again. She unlocked the door with a master key card and arched a brow at him. "You have your key, right?"

"I do." He lifted a finger toward the master in her hand. "You can just come and go?"

She shook her head, her ponytail swinging. "I would never intrude on a guest."

"Believe me, Jingles. If you let yourself into my room it wouldn't be an intrusion."

Her gaze dropped to the floor and she pushed the door open. He stepped in, and it was like he'd left the Cypress Inn behind.

Despite the inn's being quaint and full of what he guessed was Southern charm in the lobby and the dining room, his guest room was modern and comfortable and furnished like any fancy hotel up in Orlando. Ambient lighting. Clean lines. Sleek furniture. There was a small table set near a tiny fireplace done in gray tile. He caught a glimpse of a big spa-like bathroom through a doorway just beyond an enormous bed piled with pillows.

"Wow, this is really nice."

Joy beamed a smile. "Right? And I promise, no Christmas decorations unless you request them."

He stared at the top of the doorjamb. "That's a shame."

"How long are you staying, Zach?"

He shoved his hands in his front pockets. "Not really sure yet. I guess once the closing's all set I'll have to figure out what I'm going to do with the rest of my life."

Her brow furrowed a little. "I know what that's like."

"Joy, you're doing lots of stuff. None of it stick yet?"

"No."

He sat in one of the chairs at the small table. "I haven't tried anything but ranching."

"Where's Trigger and the other horses now?"

He chuckled. "Chestnut and the others are boarded at a stable in St. Cloud. I didn't want them on the property while it was being shown."

"Makes sense." She joined him, and the door shut behind her. "Maybe you could give horseback riding lessons."

He screwed up his face. "Uh, I don't think so. I'm no teacher." He thought of something she'd said when they'd first talked. "You're a teacher, right?"

"Just a substitute. What I really want to do is practice my art."

"Your art?"

Her eyes lit up and a smile broke over her face. "I'd love to create something accessible, Zach. Something people could take and live with in their homes. Something evocative."

"Evocative? Like, naked?"

She laughed. "No. I mean something that elicits feelings. Emotions."

He held up his hands. "So not my thing."

Her eyes narrowed and he wondered what she was looking for. "I think you feel more than you let on."

That confused him. "I'm an open book, Jingles."

"Nope. You're still waters, my friend. I don't think even

your brother and cousin know what makes you tick."

He conceded the point with a nod. "You might be right on that count. We're not very close."

"Billy and Chase seem close."

"They weren't always. Chase and I both gave Billy a hard time when he moved in with us."

"You were kids though, right?"

He stilled, then nodded again. "That's right, you would have heard all about it. You're in that circle."

"It's not really a circle, you know. A circle would mean it's closed off."

"That's a little deep for me."

"Sorry. Artist brain."

"So what are you working on now?"

She frowned. "Nothing. Not a darn thing."

"You're working, like, ten jobs. That's not surprising."

"I'm not blocked because I'm working, Zach. I'm working because I'm blocked."

He thought about that for a minute. "What do you do to unblock?"

She crossed her arms, looking adorably miffed in her Christmas sweater. "I have no clue."

"Maybe we can figure it out together?"

She straightened, that full mouth of hers twitching. "Are you suggesting more kissing, Zach?"

That and more, but he didn't want to send her running from the room if he shared everything he'd be willing to try.

"I can think of worse things, can't you?"

"That was purely a holiday thing."

"Was it, now?"

Her cheeks turned pink but she nodded. "Yes."

He longed to reach across the table and grab her, just to show her that his kiss had nothing to do with the holidays or a sprig of something tacked to a doorway. Nope. It was all her.

Instead, he just drank her in. She appeared flustered now, and more than a little interested.

Hopping up out of her chair, she ran her hands over her sweater. "When do you want to head out to St. Cloud?"

Right. He'd asked her to help him and to go to dinner later. Damn, he really wasn't good at this dating stuff.

"Why don't you come find me when you're finished here." He drew out his phone. "Give me your number so you'll have mine."

She recited her number and he tapped it into his phone. He

quickly texted her and heard a ding from one of the pockets in her sweater. Drawing her phone out, she deftly responded to his text.

"There." She crossed to the door. "So what are you going to do today?"

"I guess I'll get a feel for this place. I plan to stay here until Christmas, after all."

She hesitated, her hand on the door handle, and then smiled. "I'll see you later then."

He was alone a second later. Rubbing a hand over his face, he considered his options. Not for the day, since taking a tour wouldn't be any great hardship. He'd gotten his share of the development's story from a few conversations with Chase. The connection and commitment to nature was unusual for a development of its size, but he'd like to see the wilder parts of the place. It was a beautiful, though. What he'd seen of it, anyway.

He crossed to the big glass doors leading to a small balcony. He only had to take in the view of the lake to realize that the tamed yet natural landscape was like nothing he'd ever seen before.

But his options for later, when he had Joy all to himself?

The possibilities were wide open, but he wanted to taste her kisses again. That was for sure.

***

Joy whistled as she made her way toward Cool Beans, the coffee shop on the square. She'd managed to set the memory of Zach's kiss out of her mind throughout the day, since her mother had put her to work on the front desk. Calls for information and reservations had been almost nonstop. Her brother had strung even more lights in the lobby and was now putting the finishing touches on the wide veranda out front.

The decoration of the town square was clearly finished. Every lamppost and the winter-bare trees now sported twinkle lights on nearly every branch. The strains of holiday music could be heard from speakers hidden in rocks and behind bushes. The smells of cookies and peppermint seemed to cling to everything.

She closed her eyes and breathed in. This was what she liked best about Cypress. The atmosphere and the spirit that never did things half-way. And once again Zach's kiss came into her head. He didn't do things half-way either.

"That's a smile I haven't seen on your pretty face in a long time," Lettie said, breaking into Joy's reverie.

Grinning, Joy opened her eyes and faced the older woman.

"And how are you today, Lettie?"

"Apparently not as good as you are. What put that smile on your face? Or should I ask 'who?'"

Joy waved a hand. Lettie had known Joy since she was a teenager, and there was little the woman could say that would make her blush. "Just finishing up my day's work with a trip for a peppermint mocha."

"Mmm, one of my favorites. And where did you work today, busy bee?"

"At the inn." Joy came closer, stopping at her table. "Ordering bulbs, I take it?"

"Dreaming of spring, dear girl. Not that I don't love the holidays, mind you."

Joy knew that she was widowed and didn't have any children. Joy sat and placed her hand over Lettie's surprisingly supple one, given her age and the amount of gardening she did. "You're coming to the inn, aren't you Lettie? On Christmas Eve?"

"Wouldn't miss it." Lettie's blue eyes sparkled. "What about your mother's famous photo op?"

"Famous? We only did it for the first time last year."

"Still, you have to find a gentleman to play St. Nick, don't you?"

"We do." Joy narrowed her eyes. "What are you thinking?"

"Seems to me that you might have a fitting candidate living under the inn's roof."

"How did you know Zach's living at the inn?" Joy winced as she realized she'd fallen into Lettie's trap. "You got me."

Lettie laughed. "I suspected there was something between the two of you when he gave you a ride on his horse."

"That was…well, that was unexpected. That doesn't mean there's anything between us."

"Not yet."

Joy rolled her eyes. "Seeing sparks again?"

"More than sparks, Joy. You light up like a string of Christmas lights when his name is mentioned."

Joy struggled to keep her expression even. "If you say so."

"Have I ever been wrong?"

Joy didn't think so, but she wasn't going to give her the satisfaction. She just shrugged in answer.

"He's here to be closer to his family for the holiday, isn't he?" Lettie asked.

"I think so."

Lettie's expression grew thoughtful again, and Joy's senses

tingled. "He has family, Joy. Oh, maybe not as much as some folks. He could use a friend, I think."

Joy blinked at the surprising prick of tears at the back of her eyes. "I'm just helping him learn to appreciate Christmas."

Lettie tilted her head, then nodded it. "Wear that adorable elf outfit again and I think he'll do more than appreciate it."

Joy took that as her cue. "I'm going to go grab my drink. Can I get you anything?"

Lettie shook her head. "But thank you, dear."

Joy waved again and headed toward Cool Beans, mulling over what Lettie had said. Sparks? Yeah, there were sparks. He was twisted up in his feelings, though. About his family and about the ranch. And untangling that mess would be harder than unknotting the Christmas lights the time Tom had been charged with putting them away the year before.

She would text Zach after she grabbed her mocha, though. Maybe she'd even bring him one. She wouldn't touch the subject of family with him, however. It wasn't any of her business. Unless he asked her. He was her friend, right? Her hot and sexy friend who kissed her this morning like he wanted to do so much more, but still.

The bell overhead jingled as she stepped into the coffee

shop, echoing the ridiculous sweater she'd happily left back at the inn after she'd changed into more regular clothes. Worn jeans, cuffed at the ankles, and her favorite pair of red Chuck Taylors were paired with a slate blue vintage-look T-shirt over a thin thermal. It was pretty much her winter uniform, and when she added her peppermint-striped scarf she figured she was holiday enough at the moment.

There were just a few people sitting inside, but scents of coffee, caramel, peppermint and chocolate combined to make Joy's mouth water.

"Hey, there!" Grace Potter, the owner of the coffee shop, waved from her usual spot beside the big gurgling cappuccino machine. "Where's the elf outfit?"

Joy smiled and held up the ends of her scarf. "I'm doing holiday chic this afternoon. Relaxed edition."

Grace nodded, her long blond ponytail bobbing as she finished making a customer's drink. "I'm surprised your mother let you out of the house dressed like that."

Joy snorted. "Becky and Tom don't have to be little elves twenty-four seven."

"Thank god," her brother grumbled as he stepped from the back of the shop with a tray of creamer pitchers. "Hey, sis."

"Hey, little bro."

Grace set a coffee down on the pickup counter, called out the drink's details, and then wiped her hands on her brown apron as she walked back to the sales counter. "What can I get you, Joy?"

"Two peppermint mochas, Gracie. With whipped cream and sprinkles. And peppermint sticks, please."

Grace put her hands on her hips. "Two of your holiday usual? What's up?"

"Let's just say I'm bringing some holiday cheer to a friend."

"Yeah," her brother put in. "Friend."

"Did you want to say something, little brother?"

Tom stepped back from the condiment station, his hands held high. "Hey, I wasn't the one sucking face under the mistletoe this morning."

Joy's mouth dropped open. "Where were you?"

"Then he *did* see something?" Grace crossed her arms. "Do tell!"

"It seems to me that big sis here—"

"Thomas Rollins, so help me God," Joy said in her most intimidating voice.

Tom laughed, the big doofus. "Okay, sis. It wasn't like it was a make-out session or anything."

"It was a mistletoe kiss," Joy said, brushing her hair back over her shoulder. "That's all."

Tom snorted and Joy glared at him.

Grace laughed lightly. "Joy, you know your brother's mouth is set on automatic brew."

That made both Rollins siblings smile.

"Yeah," Joy said. "Love you, little bro."

Tom grinned, looking about six years old. "Love you back, big sis."

He turned and loped into the back of the shop and Joy shared a friendly glance with Grace.

"Now, about those two mochas?"

Joy shook her head. "The second one is for a friend, Gracie."

"And the mistletoe kiss?"

Joy nibbled her bottom lip. "That might have been more than a little friendly, but I'm not going to get into that now."

Grace gave a sharp nod. "Let's get together soon. Bree and Becky have been making noise about a girls' night."

"Sounds good. Just let me know."

Grace bustled around then, efficiently making Joy's order. Joy soon walked out of the coffee shop with two warm cups of holiday yumminess in her hands. She put the cups, each with a peppermint stick poking out of the lid, down on one of the iron tables in the shop's courtyard, and then drew out her phone.

All finished, she texted. *Pick me up at the coffee shop?*

Zach responded in less than a minute. *Sure thing, Jingles.*

That made her smile and she didn't care who saw it. Dropping a wink in Lettie's direction, she took the lid off one cup and sipped some peppermint mocha joy as she waited.

Chapter 7

Zach parked the truck in front of the coffee shop on the square. He spotted Joy immediately, of course. That chestnut hair of hers was down like it had been on Thanksgiving, all wavy and soft-looking, and it caught the late afternoon sunlight. She wore a striped scarf that reminded him of those sexy tights that accompanied her elf outfit.

He stepped out of the truck and nodded in Lettie's direction. "Good afternoon, ma'am."

Lettie dipped her head, her big straw hat bobbing. "Zachary."

He walked over to Joy's table and lifted his chin toward the cups in front of her. "Thirsty?"

"This one is for you, friend."

There was something about the way she called him friend that struck him as something more. Something more personal than that.

He sat across from her and set his folded arms on the table. The scent of the coffee in the cups struck him then, something like Joy and chocolate. His mouth watered.

"What is that?" he asked, leaning forward to breathe in.

She lifted the lid to reveal whipped cream and a candy

cane. "For you. Peppermint mocha, extraordinaire."

He wrinkled his nose and brought the cup to his lips. "How do I even drink this?"

"Slowly, Zach." She dipped her candy stick in her whipped cream and licked it. "Indulgent holiday goodness."

He stared at her lips, her tongue, and nearly groaned. "You'll get on the naughty list if you keep doing that, Jingles."

She laughed, her cheeks turning pink. "Drink your coffee, Zach. Then tell me if you don't have at least a little more of the Christmas spirit."

Zach sipped, finding the drink almost as delicious as Joy's kiss had been. "Okay, maybe a little."

Her eyes sparkled with apparent humor.

"What?" he asked.

"Moustache, Zach."

He licked his lips, and saw that she watched his mouth now. Popping the lid back on his coffee, he stood. "Let's take our, what did you call them? Indulgent holiday goodness? On the road."

She nodded. "Sounds good."

They each lifted their cups in Lettie's direction and headed for his truck. He opened the door and she climbed in. Her worn jeans hugged her long, shapely legs and her sneakers were a cute surprise.

"I thought we'd head to the ranch first, if that's okay," he said.

"Sure." She sipped at her coffee, purring with pleasure. "I'm at your disposal."

He nodded. "I have to pick up a few things to take to the inn."

"You're really staying until Christmas?"

"Yep."

"And you won't miss being in your family home for the holiday?"

His belly gave a strange twist. "Not even a little bit."

She wore a thoughtful expression as she sipped at her drink. The drive wasn't a long one, and before long they were turning up the dusty road toward the Harris ranch.

Joy straightened in her seat, leaning slightly to peer out the windshield. "I've never been in this part of St. Cloud."

"This is the outskirts, really." He maneuvered the truck over the rutted road, grateful it hadn't rained in a few days. "It's not like the state-named streets of the city or the main shopping areas, I know."

"It's so…rustic."

"It is that." The ranch house came into view, set back from the road about one hundred feet. "The cattle and horses sure like it."

She gave a shiver, and he remembered how nervous she'd been around Chestnut. "I don't see any animals."

"They roam free, more or less. The horses are boarded in St. Cloud."

He waited for a flicker of homesickness or even fondness for the sturdy, simply home. It was large, but that was probably the best thing he could say about it. It was serviceable, and looked like a typical ranch house.

"Wow, Zach. Your house is amazing."

"It's big."

"Okay, I'll give you that."

The gravel on the drive crunched as he pulled the truck to a stop not far from the wide front porch. He cranked off the engine and sat back. Memories came to him. His father gone to the stables or out in the fields as his mother sat alone on the porch. Chase had been very young but Zach had known that something wasn't right. He'd had no clue she was going to leave, though. How the hell could he?

"Zach?"

Joy's voice reached him and he turned to find her looking at him, her eyes dark. She was real. Warm and alive, and he had no business looking at the cold dead memories of his childhood in a house that soon wasn't even going to be his.

"Come on," he said, his voice gruff. "I promise this won't take long."

She stepped out of the truck before he could reach her side, and then walked up to the big empty porch. "It's no wonder you sold this place so quickly. It looks like something out of a movie."

"An old movie." He stepped up and took her hand, that felt natural but he wasn't going to think about that right now, and pulled her around to the back side of the porch. "All that land, Jingles? That's Harris land. Or, it was."

She gaped at the wide open space. He figured it could be considered a little surprising to see all of that land so close to the city. Not that St. Cloud was a metropolis, but the houses in the city limits were all set very close together. Out here, the nearest neighbor was over a mile away in either direction.

"How much land is this?" she asked, dropping his hand to stand near the porch railing.

"About seven hundred acres. It was a lot larger when my father was a kid, but he sold it off as developers moved in. It's been this size for as long as I can remember, though."

She turned back to him. "What do you have, like a thousand cows?"

He chuckled. "Cattle, and no. We have about one hundred and fifty. Only eight horses right now, though."

"Eight is plenty."

He stepped up to her. "You like Chestnut now, don't you?"

"He's all right."

He nudged her with his shoulder. "Good thing he's boarded with the others, then."

"I think it might be."

He unlocked the back door and they entered the kitchen. She peered into a few of the cabinets, which were still full of plates and things.

"You have a lot of packing to do." She placed her hands on her hips. "Is that why you lured me out here?"

He laughed. "Not even close."

Her eyes sparkled again and he closed the gap between them. Holding her close, his hands at the small of her back, he could feel every curve.

"Zach, what are you doing?"

"Thinking about kissing you."

She licked her lips. "There's no mistletoe."

He brushed her lips with his, breathing in her scent. "We'll have to improvise."

She stilled for a second, and then placed her hands on each side of his head. "The heck with it."

She kissed him, full on the mouth. She parted her lips and he drove his tongue inside to tangle with hers. Making a sweet sound of surrender, she seemed to melt against him. His heart raced as he kissed her throat, flicking his tongue over the tender hollow.

"Oh, my," she sighed.

He had his hands on her ass, one cheek in each, and pulled her tight against him. How could a simple kiss turn so hot so quickly?

Releasing her, he leaned back and let out a breath.

***

Zach seemed unwilling to let go of her completely, though. He kept his hands at her waist.

"That's not why I lured you out here, either," he said.

She stared up at him, her lips parted as her breath came

fast. "That's too bad."

His eyes glittered and one corner of his mouth curved. He had to know she was kidding. She wasn't a hit-it-and-quit-it kind of woman.

"Don't tempt me, Jingles," he said, stepping away at last. "The buyers want it all, so except for my personal belongings, everything is staying right where it is."

"You don't have anything you want to keep? Family mementoes or heirlooms?"

He shrugged. "Chase is coming out here with Carrie to see if she wants anything. We have a chance to negotiate if she decides she can't live without some of this old junk."

Joy looked around, her nose wrinkled. "There really isn't much here. You said this was in the family for how long?"

"Don't know. My father grew up here."

She tilted her head. "You don't know its history?"

"Not even a little bit. Don't look so surprised. If you'd known Wild Harry, you would understand."

Recognition dawned on her. "Is that where you get the strong, silent vibe?"

"I guess so."

She closed the cabinet door. "Then let's get going. You

promised me dinner and that mocha only whet my appetite."

He caught her in his arms as she passed him, planting a quick kiss on her full mouth. "Mine, too."

As they walked through the house she could read a dispassionate expression on his face. His features were even and there wasn't a touch of melancholy as he ticked off the contents of the rooms out loud.

"Do you think Carrie would want this sofa?" he asked.

Joy eyed the monstrous plaid couch and visibly shuddered. "I would be stunned if she did."

That startled a laugh out of him. "Okay, then. Let's go upstairs."

By the time they finished going through the family bedrooms, it was clear to Joy that this was really just a house. It wasn't a home by any stretch. Even the room he'd identified as his own bore very few personal touches. It was neat and simple, and suited him very well. He stuffed a duffel bag with clothes as she wandered over to the small bookcase set beneath the windows that overlooked the sprawling ranch.

It was a boy's bookcase, painted dark blue and holding a few baseball trophies and stacks of thin books. There was a framed picture there on the middle shelf, tucked behind a

Rubik's Cube and a deck of playing cards. There were two little boys in the photo, with a woman that had to be Zach's mother. There was a resemblance there, and though the woman was very pretty there was a sadness in her blue eyes.

"I guess that's enough for now," he said, zipping the duffle shut.

"Did you want this?" she asked, holding out the frame.

He paled, and then his cheeks glowed red. "Uh…"

"Never mind," she said, quickly setting it back on the shelf.

"No, that's okay." He sucked in an audible breath and straightened. "That's me and Chase, before our mother left."

Joy stuck her hands in her back pockets, rocking a little in her sneakers. "I figured that was who it was." She paused a beat. "I'd heard that she left, Zach. From Carrie. I didn't know you were so young, though."

He ran a hand through his hair. "It's no biggie." He took the picture frame, keeping his gaze from it as he opened the duffle bag and shoved it inside. "The buyers aren't going to want it."

Joy looked at the rest of the contents of the bookcase. "Did you want anything else from here? Like these, maybe?"

He swiped at his eye and cleared his throat. "What?" Walking over, he picked up the trophies. "I guess they wouldn't want these, either."

"Take them, Zach. You'll regret it if you don't."

"If you say so." The words were light but his tone was flat. Still, he took the two trophies from her and then grabbed the third one from the shelf. "I forgot I'd left these here."

She was fairly confident he was telling the truth. "I wondered why there weren't any posters of race cars or hot girls from your teenage years."

"Swept the place of all that stuff years ago." He put the trophies in the bag and finally gave her a small smile. "I think I prefer having a flesh and blood hot girl here instead."

She just shook her head. "Flatterer."

He shouldered the bag and took a look around. "Let's go, Jingles."

He waved her ahead of him and they went back downstairs. He was quiet as he drove away from the ranch, but as they put a few miles between them and his family home he seemed to relax those big shoulders of his.

"Hot wings, cold beer and a few games of pool," he said as they pulled into the parking lot of the End Zone.

"That sounds just about perfect," she said.

The sports bar apparently did a good business on a Tuesday night, judging by the usual assortment of jacked-up trucks and chrome-encrusted Harleys in the lot. Zach parked and they went in.

The interior was dim but the large dining room to the right was lined all around with TVs set high on the walls broadcasting fishing shows and Ultimate Fighting matches. A country/pop song played from the digital jukebox and the scent of French fries and buffalo wings hung in the air. There were few families seated at the wooden tables and booths, but plenty of couples and pairs of couples. The singles? They appeared to be hugging the long bar at the back of the cavernous space.

"Sit anywhere you like," a fast-moving server with a swinging blond ponytail said over her shoulder.

Zach urged Joy ahead of him as they made their way toward a booth set against one wall. They slid inside across from each other and, although the place was crowded, the booth had an intimate feel. The wood paneling was dark and the seatbacks tall.

She thought about what Lettie had said about him needing his family, and wondered just what the woman knew about him.

Her knowledge of everyone in the Cypress fishbowl was legendary. Maybe she'd heard something from Shannon or Carrie about the way the Harris men had grown up. The ranch house wasn't only furnished with a nod to comfort and serviceability, there wasn't a single touch of hominess. And certainly no femininity.

Another server, this one with black hair and a lot of eyeliner, stopped at their table. "What can I get you." The woman yelped, and then laughed. "Zach Harris! Long time, no see."

Joy watched as a blush crawled up Zach's chiseled cheeks.

"Hey, Mandy," Zach said, folding his hands and keeping his eyes on the scarred tabletop. "I'll have a Bud, please. Bottle."

Joy looked over at the server, seeing an arch expression on the woman's face. "Make that two?"

The server looked between her and Zach, apparently seeing something she herself was only just beginning to. There was an attraction between them. Some kind of connection, though they'd only known each other a few days. There was the matter of that incredible kiss in his kitchen, though.

"Sure." The woman seemed to be waiting and Zach finally looked up at her. "Nice to see you."

"You, too," Zach said.

She seemed satisfied by his acknowledgment and turned toward the bar to get their drinks. Mandy came back with their beers and Zach ordered some hot wings. The server seemed unaffected now, and clearly there weren't any lingering feelings for Zach that Joy could see.

Still, Zach shook his head. "Sorry about that," he said, his voice low.

"Nothing to be sorry for." She thought she'd tease him a little, and get him to relax those broad shoulders of his. "Unless you've been kissing her under the mistletoe, too?"

His brows arched and a sexy smile curved his tempting mouth. "No worries, Jingles. I haven't kissed anybody else in months, mistletoe or not."

For some reason that warmed her more than the peppermint mocha had. Setting aside jealous server girls and odd family dynamics, she decided to focus on having an easy night out with the hottest guy she knew.

Getting smiles out of him was a challenge she happily accepted. Any day of the week.

Chapter 8

Zach drained his beer and leaned back in the booth. After a rocky start to their, he guessed this was a date, Joy seemed to grow more comfortable. He sure had. Seeing Mandy had been a surprise, though it shouldn't have been. She'd been working here for the last year at least. He hadn't slept with her for almost as long, but from the way she'd reacted to seeing him with Joy it seemed like she held at least a little ill will towards him.

"I'm stuffed." Joy folded her arms and sighed. "Those were probably the best wings I've had in forever. And the most, too."

"Yeah, they make a good wing."

She arched a brow, a smile playing around her mouth. "Okay. Now are you going to talk about little miss hook-up over there?"

"I haven't been with her in over a year, Joy." He thought she could use a little more truth from him. "Hell, I haven't been with anybody in nearly that long."

"That's surprising."

"What, do you think I'm a hound dog or something?"

"No." Her eyes sparkled and he realized she was teasing him. "I'm just saying that you're pretty easy on the eyes,

Cowboy."

He chuckled. "That's fair, and nice of you to say."

She held up her hands. "Oh come on, Zach. You and your brother and cousin have a combined heat rating of well over a thousand degrees. White hot, maybe? I don't think I could even recreate that color."

"White?" He smirked. "Not much of an artist, then."

Something flickered in her eyes, gone in a second. "I guess I should probably come up with something for the holiday festival. At least for the kids' event."

"When is that?"

"Haven't you looked at *The Cypress Scoop* my mother leaves for guests in the lobby?"

"The what?"

"The weekly, hmm. Newspaper is a pretty generous name for it. No?"

He shook his head and her eyes narrowed.

"What about the official event calendar we slip under every door every morning?" she asked.

"I haven't woken up at the inn yet, Jingles."

"You're excused, then. All of the upcoming events, and photos of the previous ones, are in the paper."

"I'll have to check it out, then. You said you teach. Do you like working with kids?"

She nodded, her face brightening. "I do, but I'd hoped working with the kids at the community school would spark something inside of me."

"Something? Like what, art?"

"Yeah." She blew out a breath and the expression on her face was one of regret and frustration. "I've got nothing, Zach. Bupkis. Zip."

"What kind of art did you used to, I guess the word is make? At school?"

"Mostly painting. Some acrylic, some oil. I also worked with different media, like paper."

"Chase and I used to make paper airplanes." He blinked. "I don't know why I thought of that."

"Nostalgia. Maybe from being in your old bedroom today."

He snorted. "I was in that bedroom just yesterday, Joy. And for a long damn time before that. Nothing grabbed me then."

"Maybe it was the picture of your mother," she said in a soft voice.

A twist came to his gut, a little sick feeling, and he shook his head. "I'm not a nostalgic kind of guy. I guess I get that from my father."

"I didn't see any family pictures downstairs. I thought maybe you got rid of them over the years."

He shook his head. "Nope. Wild Harry never kept any pictures around. I don't remember seeing any before my mother left, but who knows? I was just a kid. Pretty self-involved, I guess."

"Like most kids should be." She leaned forward. "I'll let you in on a little secret."

He felt a curl of something way better than that coldness hit his belly now. "That sounds promising."

She smiled and wrinkled her nose. "I have no clue about what I want to do."

"You want to make art. That's clear every time you talk about it. You light up."

Her brows arched. "Do I? Hmm. Now if I could just channel some of that light into my work. Heck, into any work but the jobs I'm doing now. That's about all this is, really. All of it. Busy work."

"We do what we have to. At least you weren't chained to a place you couldn't wait to get rid of."

Her mouth dropped open. Zach nearly bit his tongue. Where the hell had that come from?

"You've sold the ranch, Zach. You'll be free of it soon."

Her hand covered his fist on the table, and he realized he'd been clenching his hands for the last few minutes. Since talk of his childhood on the ranch, really.

"It was a good life, Joy. I'm grateful for what my father left me."

"He left Billy a lot of money too, right?" She shrugged before he could get out an answer. "I know that was his stake for his goat farm."

"Yep. I don't begrudge Billy his inheritance. Chase and me, we got to share the ranch."

"I can't imagine growing up on a ranch. Your place is beautiful."

"I do love the land."

"Are you going to miss the cows?" She flashed a smile. "I'm sorry. Cattle?"

"Nah. My father had known cattle, and Chase and me had learned enough of the business side of things to turn the ranch into a moneymaker. I'm more about the horses."

"Tell me about the stables you're going to build, then."

"I don't know how involved I'll be."

She tilted her head. "Won't your horses live there?"

"I hadn't thought about it." He brushed a hand through his hair. "Maybe."

Mandy came by the table again. "Would you two like anything else?"

He looked over at Joy who shook her head. "Nah, we're set. Just the check, Mandy."

Mandy nodded, all business as she brought the check back to their table.

"So, Jingles." He leaned back and crossed his arms. "You about ready for that game of pool now?"

She clasped her hands and slid out of the booth. "Prepare yourself, Cowboy. I've been trained by the best."

He came to his feet. "Do I want to know?"

"Claire Chapman, Zach. You know the Chapmans, right?"

Zach shrugged. "They founded Cypress, right?"

She laughed, that light sound he really liked to hear. "No, but over the last few years they've all settled down here. Claire is married to Jake Chapman."

"He's the guy that runs the Adventure Trails, right?"

She shook her head. "Of course you'd know about those.

Have you run them?"

"Not a triathlon, but I've hit the running trails. You?"

"I run, but it's not my favorite. I like to do yoga, though."

He had a quick picture in his head of her supple body stretched and twisted into all sorts of interesting positions. She must have seen something in his expression, because she lightly punched him in the arm.

"Mind out of the gutter," she said. "And into the pool room."

Chuckling, he followed her through the dining area and under the big archway leading to the pool room. This was a little strange for him. This kidding around and hanging out with a woman. Joy wasn't just any woman, though. He'd sensed that on Thanksgiving. He wasn't quite sure what she was, or what she could be to him.

And for the first time in his memory, he really wanted to find out. Also for the first time? He was certain he'd do something to fuck this up long before the New Year.

***

The inn was quiet when Joy and Zach returned around ten. All of the guests, and her mother and Tom apparently, must be up in their rooms. The gas fireplace was still flickering behind the glass screen in the front parlor though, and it beckoned her as they shook off the chill of the damp night air.

"All the children were nestled," she said in a whisper, unwrapping her scarf from her neck.

Zach's brows rose. "Huh?"

She stifled a laugh. "The poem, Zach?" At his blank expression she chuckled. She couldn't help it. "The Night Before Christmas?"

He blinked, and then his pretty blue eyes twinkled. "I know, Jingles. I'm just pulling your twinkly lights."

She smiled, pleased to see this teasing side of him. His smile was as gorgeous as the rest of him. "Let's sit by the fire?"

"Lead the way." Zach placed his hand on the small of her back, the light touch sending a flush over her body. He leaned closer to her, his lips close enough to her ear to make her tremble. "You owe me a rematch, by the way."

She glanced over her shoulder at him and grinned. She'd managed to surprise him a couple of times while they played pool, using the tricks Claire Chapman had taught her. Claire was a CPA and the money mind of Cypress, and a true math geek. Joy could admit to herself that she'd been lost on most of Claire's tutelage, but using her tips to clear the pool table a few times actually made the thought of math fun.

"Are you saying you're sorry I whipped your butt?" she asked as she settled down on the thickly-upholstered couch angled near the fireplace.

He shook his head and sat beside her, his leg touching hers. "Not in the least. I figure it leaves me indebted to you."

Something occurred to her, then. Something that Lettie had suggested. "Hmm. Are you game, Zach?"

"Game?" He rested his arm on the back of the couch behind her. "Are you trying to get me on the naughty list, Jingles?"

For a second, she wanted to push him down under the Christmas tree and do all sorts of naughty things to him. She licked her lips, longing for a taste of his kisses from earlier, and shook her head. "This is more about the nice list, Cowboy."

He nuzzled her cheek, his stubble scraping ever so lightly over her neck. "Mmm, nice." He grabbed her earlobe with his teeth for a second, and then sat back. "Okay, I'll bite."

"Ha, funny guy." She turned a little to face him, doing her best not to get distracted by the flicker of firelight over his shoulder. The spark of heat in his eyes. "I wondered if you would do something for me? Um, for us?"

His brows drew together. "What kind of something?"

She bit her lower lip, and then shrugged. "Can you be our Santa?"

His eyes rounded, and he threw his head back and laughed.

"Shh," she said, chuckling herself. "My mother's room is on this floor. Besides, you'll wake all the mice."

He nodded, a smile curving his lips. "I get it. Not a creature… But I have to ask. Why me?"

"Lettie suggested it, but it would really work out for me. My mother wanted to get another guy, this curmudgeon from the design committee."

"What's wrong with him?"

"Nothing, really. At least he wouldn't need padding for the suit. He's just such a blowhard."

"And I'm laid-back, is that what you're saying?"

She gave a slow shake of her head. "You might look easygoing, but I know you're still waters."

He shifted, coming closer to her. He placed his free hand on her hip, his touch just right. "What will you give me in return?"

She put her hands on his big, broad shoulders. "I'll stuff your stocking?"

He brought his mouth to hers. "Ah, Jingles. You're putting all sorts of naughty ideas in my head."

She brought her face to his, breathing in his fresh and hot scent. "What?" She brushed her lips against his beautifully-sculpted mouth. "You'll want a snow job?"

He nipped at her lips, then grinned. "Not the kind of job I might have asked for, but sure." He looked away for a second, the firelight catching on his perfect profile. He was almost in silhouette, and something sparked inside of her. She wanted to freeze the moment, and the feeling was startling.

"Zach," she whispered, bringing him back to her. She leaned closer and his arms wrapped around her now. "Kiss me, Zach. No mistletoe. No nostalgia. Just me."

"Ah, Joy." He ran his hands over her back. "I've been dying to do that since this afternoon at the ranch."

His mouth was hungry on hers, and she welcomed his tongue. He tasted as wild as the outdoors and more delicious than a peppermint mocha. He pulled away slightly, running his tongue over her throat as her breath quickened. His hands, those big hands of his, grabbed her butt and drew her even closer. She wanted to be under him in that second. To have his tall, broad body all over her.

"Upstairs, baby." He kissed her neck, dragging her sweater down to reveal one shoulder. "I'll ring your bells, I promise."

This naughty, funny side of him was as seductive as his magical touch. She leaned back, bringing her hand to his cheek.

"I want to, Zach. It's just too soon."

His nostrils flared as he breathed in, and then he gave a short nod. "I get it." He stood, taking her hand and pulling her to her feet. "Then at least I can walk you home."

"I am home."

"To your room, Jingles."

She grabbed her scarf and followed him up to the second floor. When he made for the next set of stairs, she tugged on his hand.

"You're up there, Zach." She lifted her chin down the hallway in front of them. "I'm down here. In steerage, so to speak."

"I doubt your mother has any rooms that aren't pretty nice."

"It's nice," she said. "Just smaller than the ones on the top floor."

"No balcony?"

"Nope." She led him down the hall to her door at the very

end. "Here we are."

He pressed close to her, framing her head with his hands on the wall behind her. "Good night, then."

He kissed her, and in a flash her pulse raced and her knees were as soft as toasted marshmallows. Then he stepped back, leaving her holding onto the wall for support.

"Good night, Zach," she breathed.

He dropped a wink and walked away from her. As he reached the staircase, he turned back to her. "And I'll be your Santa, Jingles."

"You will?" She gaped at him. "Why?"

He chuckled, the sound low and wrapping around her. "For that snow job."

She was laughing as she let herself into her small room. He was her Santa, and he had just nearly become her lover. Did she want that? He had issues, and she wasn't exactly in a place to help him work his way through his stuff. No. She was mired in her own brand of it, and it was as sticky as an old candy cane.

He could kiss, though. And probably was just as good at all of the other stuff. Goodness knew she hadn't had any of that other stuff in a very long time.

She thought about that flash of something she'd felt as

she'd gazed at his silhouette. There was something there, beyond his obvious masculine beauty. She walked over to the small desk by the window, ignoring her boxes of things she'd dragged home from UCF. There were a few sharpened pencils in the painted box set on the desk, and a few pieces of Cypress Inn stationery in the shallow top drawer.

Flipping one piece over, she began to sketch. It was funny, since she'd known Zach for such a short time, but she could see his face in her mind. She did a quick drawing, but it didn't grab her. It was him all right, but it didn't capture the beauty of his silhouette backlit by the fire.

It struck her then, like an icy snowball to the face.

"Duh!" She laughed to herself. "Joy Rollins, you're an idiot."

It wasn't ideal, since the stationery was thicker than the special glossy paper meant for silhouette cutting. Her boxes were labeled, of course. She was her mother's daughter. Her art supplies were neatly packed, and she located the tiny scissors right away.

Humming to herself, she began to shape the paper into Zach's profile. It wasn't perfect, given the paper and the lack of the subject sitting in front of her. This was something she'd always loved to do, though. As a bit of a palate cleanser between larger projects. It could be just what she needed. Just what she would do to create the very thing she'd told Zach about back in his room. Something accessible. Evocative. Had that only been this morning?

She began to go through her boxes, humming Christmas carols as she searched for the special paper with an urgency she hadn't felt in months.

Chapter 9

Joy was dressed as an elf again the next morning, but she didn't even mind the pointy-toed shoes as she danced down the staircase. Last night with Zach had been so much fun. Letting go was something she hadn't done in so darn long, and it was really freeing.

Cutting his silhouette had done something for her, too. She'd accomplished a few things very early this morning, and only hoped that she wasn't being too impulsive. It felt right, though. Like she was forcing herself to rely on her God-given (according to her father) and well-earned (according to her mother) talents.

"Joy, there you are!" her mother said, as she did pretty much every single morning.

"Good morning, Mom." Joy walked over to where her mother stood refilling the coffee pot, the bells on her skirt ringing happily. "What can I do?"

Her mother stopped what she was doing, spilling a few drops of coffee on the polished wood tabletop. "What?"

Joy dipped her head, taking a breath before she met her mother's probing gaze. "I'm at your disposal, Mom. I'm not working anywhere else."

Her mother's mouth dropped open. "Really?" Then she smiled, her eyes lit. "Oh, Joy!"

They both laughed at the inadvertent pun.

"I called the tavern and quit. Told them I have too many demands for the holidays." She placed her hands on her hips and lifted one shoulder. "They didn't seem too put out. I guess I'm not exactly integral to their everyday operation."

Her mother clasped her hands with hers. "Oh, dear! I'm so happy. You know, your sister is so busy with her career and Tom is still finding himself."

Joy figured she landed somewhere in between her siblings, so she nodded. "If a sub day comes up at the school, I'll want to pick it up but I'm going to be all about the inn and the holiday festival."

"The festivals, Joy. The first one is next week!"

"I know." She scanned the dining room now, looking but not finding Zach. "I think I found a Santa, at least."

"Oh?" Her mother wiped the spill and faced Joy again. "I thought we were going with Johnny?"

"Nope. I asked Zach Harris to step in."

"That's wonderful!" She stared to say something else, but then looked over Joy's shoulder. "He'll be just perfect, with the right costume of course."

Joy felt Zach before she saw him. That electric buzz that seemed to flow between them, and his yummy fresh scent, made her want to grin. Her mother was watching closely though, so she just nodded and turned.

"St. Nick, I presume?" she asked.

He smiled at her mother and then turned a wicked look in Joy's direction. "I'm ready to fill those stockings."

Joy choked on a laugh but her mother just giggled.

"Mr. Harris, thank you so much!" She took Zach's elbow and led him toward the breakfast table. "Our first photo op is this weekend, you know. Then there's the festival starting on Friday of next week. Just about a week from today!"

Zach nodded to her mother's instructions and Joy just poured herself a cup of coffee. Maybe she'd ask Zach to drive into town with her today. She needed to go to the art supply store in St. Cloud, and could use his strong arms to lug all of her supplies. Not really, since her supplies shouldn't weigh very much at all. His arms would look pretty nice doing that lugging, though.

She sipped at her coffee in a to-go cup, deciding that she would stop by Cool Beans on her way out of Cypress this afternoon. This stuff her mother brewed just didn't do it for her. Maybe she'd stop by the bakery, too. Caro Graham always came up with something new for the holiday festivals, and Joy doubted this year would be the exception. Her pumpkin spice biscotti had stolen the show again at this year's fall festival. Joy was thinking about that almond peppermint cookie of hers right now, though.

"What's on your plate today, Joy?" Zach asked as he helped himself to a cinnamon roll.

"I'm going to be my mother's personal elf, Zach. At least until this afternoon."

He nodded, making his way over to what she was rapidly beginning to think of as their table. "Join me, Jingles."

"Yes, I know." She flounced over, her bells ringing, and sat. "I look ridiculous."

His eyes flared. "You look adorable and hot, something I'd noticed when I saw you on the side of the road."

She sipped her plain coffee and shook her head. "That sounds like the beginning of a country song, Cowboy."

He chuckled, and boy did she love when he did that. His low laugh was a little rough and made her think things that had nothing to do with Christmas.

"I'm meeting with the realtor this morning, to go over the list of things Chase wants to keep."

"You spoke with him about the furniture?"

"Yep. Seems he has a lot more sentimental attachment to that stuff than I do. He emailed me the list. You're free, when? After three again?"

"I should be. I have a few things to pick up in St. Cloud. Want to come with me?"

"Need my strong arms, do you?"

She studied those arms, showcased by the rolled-up sleeves of his gray chambray shirt. "Mmm hmm."

He leaned closer. "What are you thinking about?"

She blinked, her cheeks hot. "What?"

"You get all sparkly sometimes, Jingles. And I don't mean twinkly lights."

She fiddled with her coffee cup, her eyes on the tabletop. "I was thinking about those strong arms holding me up last night, if you must know."

"I think I do." He crossed said arms and sat back. "What do you need in St. Cloud?"

She nibbled her bottom lip before answering, almost afraid to say it out loud. "I need some art supplies."

He cocked his head to the side. What was he looking for? The answer to what she was meant to be? His gaze was full of expectation, but that was nothing compared to what she wanted for herself.

"You had yourself a burst of inspiration there, did you?" he teased.

She snorted. "Okay, fine. Something about the firelight and a certain cowboy got me thinking."

He straightened a little. "Now, that sounds interesting. Thinking about what, exactly?"

"Paper."

"You said you worked with paper. I don't get it, but I don't think I'm supposed to."

"Not yet, anyway." She blew out a breath. "I'm going to start creating, Zach. Something, anyway. I want to have a booth at the first holiday festival next week."

"You should do it, Jingles. I think it should be a kissing booth, but what do I know?"

She laughed out loud, then shook her head at him. "That's a sharp sense of humor you keep hidden under all of that brooding, Cowboy."

He finished his pastry and stood. "I'm off to meet the

realtor down at the coffee shop."

"Out here?"

"It's where I live now, isn't it?"

Joy's mouth gaped. "I guess it is."

He glanced around the dining room, and then leaned down to kiss her quickly on the lips. "Later, Jingles. Text me."

She sat there with her lukewarm coffee in its soggy cup, thinking about what he'd said. He lived here in Cypress now? It was an about-face from where he'd been just last week.

He was cutting himself loose from his ties to his family's ranch and, despite the touch of reluctance she'd seen that night he and his family had come to the tavern, it was something that was apparently long overdue. He didn't talk much about his father, or his mother for that matter, and Joy wasn't going to press him on the subject. No. Today she was going to do something to get him into the spirit when they drove into town. Hopefully that would help her foster the artist's nature he'd jumpstarted at long last.

***

Zach sat in Cool Beans, sipping an Americano. The tall redheaded kid behind the counter of the coffee shop had recommended it. He'd seen Tom around the inn, actually. It was clear he was Joy's little brother even if Zach had never set eyes on him before.

He'd been lucky to get a table, actually. The shop did a brisk business, with an almost-constant line of caffeine junkies. The sound of chatter was kind of nice, though. And the place was filled with the scents of coffee, chocolate and a dash of peppermint. That was quickly becoming his favorite scent.

"Mr. Harris, hello!"

He turned to find the realtor smiling at him. He rose in his seat as she sat across from him. "Good morning. Can I get you a coffee or something?"

She waved a hand, and then brushed her curly brown hair back from her face. "No, I can't stay. I have an interview over at the Sales Center in a little while."

"You're going to work out here?"

She beamed a smile at him. "Cypress is hot, Mr. Harris. And I don't just mean the guys I've seen running around this place."

Zach shrugged. "If you say so."

She laughed and then put her messenger bag on the table. "I'll get this information to the buyers." Looking over the list, she gave a slow nod. "There doesn't seem to be a lot on here.

They were prepared to negotiate the bulk of the items, so I doubt they'll take much off of their offer."

"I'm mainly interested in the tack and other things from the stables, miss."

"Call me Darby. Please."

"Darby. My brother and his wife made that list of the household stuff."

"No matter. I'll make sure you keep what you want to."

Zach felt a sense of relief at her words. "Thanks, Darby."

She slid the document into her bag, folding her hands on top of the leather. "Do you like living out here, Mr. Harris?"

"Zach, and I think so. I'm staying at the inn, so it's more like I'm living at the North Pole."

"I saw that! I admit, I'm a sucker for Christmas."

"Then you have to come to the festivals."

"Oh, I'll be there. Hopefully I'll have a position out here by then." She came to her feet. "Wish me luck. I'm meeting with Rick Chapman at eleven."

Zach nodded. "I'm sure you'll get it."

She blew a curl off of her forehead. "Thank you for that. I'll be in touch!"

With that, she left the coffee shop. He'd heard about Rick,

mainly from Chase. His brother said the guy was a straight-shooter despite being from Boston. Seems there were a few people from that neck of the woods. Carrie had said that both Eli Graham and Derek Stone, two guys who work at the Sales Center, were from up north too.

"Do you want a biscotti or something, Mr. Harris?" Tom asked him as he wiped down a nearby table. Two people slid into its chairs the second Tom was finished.

"Call me Zach, Tom."

The kid flashed a smile that looked a lot like Joy's. "Zach."

"And no thanks."

Tom leaned down. "Don't let my boss hear, but you can't beat the stuff they make over at Sweet Escape."

"I heard that!" the blond woman behind the counter teased. "It's bad enough that Caro stole you away from me to teach you how to bake."

"It's only a couple of days a week, Gracie."

"Humph."

Tom looked back at Zach. "I hear you're helping out with the photo op?"

"Word travels fast."

"Cypress, my man." Tom spread his arms wide. "The

fishbowl."

"Your sister mentioned something about that."

The kid looked like he wanted to say something more, like maybe ask Zach just what his intentions were toward his sister or something like that, but the coffee shop owner called him over.

"Okay!" He smiled at Zach. "I'll see you at home, I guess."

The kid's words struck him in the gut. Was this home now? *How the hell did that happen?*

Yeah, he was selling the ranch. Yeah, he had nowhere else to go. There was something pulling at him here, though. He could admit that to himself. It had to do with comfort, sure. And a hominess the ranch house had never possessed. But it was more than that. His feelings about Cypress were all tied up with a big red Christmas bow, and ringed with twinkly lights. The reason for it all could be laid at a certain hot little elf's pointy shoes.

The bell over the door jingled at that second, and he nearly jumped. Smiling to himself, he drained his coffee and stood.

"Thanks," he said to the blond.

"Thank you," she said, glancing over from her spot at the register.

Zach stepped outside, looking up and down the street

bracketing the pretty town square. Cypress was a nice place. He couldn't deny that. He had family here now, and soon there wouldn't be anything tying him to St. Cloud or his father's legacy. The horses, maybe. Harry had known horses almost as well as he knew cattle, and the few good conversations Zach had with him over the years had concerned stock and breeding and how to choose the perfect horse for each rider.

He smiled absently at a strawberry blond woman pushing a stroller and stuck his hands in his front pockets. Joy had suggested he give horseback riding lessons. He wasn't sure about how great a teacher he'd be, but he knew a lot about the animals. At the very least he could ask Billy if he thought the stables might support lessons.

As if on cue, his phone rang. It was his cousin Billy.

"Hey, cuz," he answered.

"Hey, Zach," Billy said. "Can you come out here tomorrow? I've been thinking about the stables we talked about last week."

"Sure. What are you thinking?"

"I want us to partner on them. I think they could be a big hit out here."

Zach's belly clenched. This would be another tie to this

place. He wasn't even sure if he wanted that, but he owed Billy at least a conversation about the possibility.

"Uh, okay. What time?"

"Shannon and I are up with the dawn, man." He heard the laughter in Billy's voice. "Come out in the morning any time you like."

"Cool, I will."

"Later."

Billy disconnected and Zach clutched the phone. He wasn't sure what his future was, but he knew he couldn't drag his feet any longer. He'd meet with Billy, give him his advice, and then let him take it from there. As for partnering? He wasn't sure about that, either.

He pocketed his phone and realized then that he'd walked the square only to return to the coffee shop. Lettie Fairfax waved him over, and Zach thought he'd oblige her.

"Good morning, Lettie."

"Good morning, Zachary. How does this day find you? Jolly, I'd bet?"

Zach barked out a laugh. "So you've heard?"

She smiled up at him. "I have indeed. Joy wasted no time, did she?"

Zach thought about the time he'd spent with Joy and silently agreed that none of it had been wasted. "No, she didn't."

Lettie crossed her arms. "And how does the sale of your ranch go? I hear you and your brother will be sitting pretty once all is said and done."

Now that was a surprise. "How do you know about that?"

Lettie blushed a little and her gaze fell to her seed magazines. "That sweet little Darby from St. Cloud might have mentioned it."

Zach doubted that. The realtor had been completely professional in all of her dealings with him. There was no way she would tell somebody out here about their private business.

"Really."

Lettie forced a laugh and waved a hand. "Oh, I might have just heard something around town."

"Zach!" Joy called from down the street.

He turned in Joy's direction and waved, willing to let go of his interrogation of Lettie for a moment. She didn't seem to have a bad bone, so he dipped his head to her.

"I'm being summoned, ma'am."

Lettie smiled with obvious relief. "Go get your elf, Santa."

He saw that Joy still wore her elf costume, so Lettie wasn't too far off. As for her being his? That was something he could admit he'd felt from the jump.

"Zach, I got it!" She flung herself into his arms and he happily caught her.

"I don't know what you're talking about," he said close to her ear. "But congratulations."

She stepped back, beaming up at him. She was practically shaking with excitement. "I have a booth of my own at the festival."

"A kissing booth?"

She swatted his arm. "My art booth. At both festivals, if the first one is a success."

"Are you going to tell me about this art, Jingles? Or am I to wait for the unveiling?"

She tilted her head, her ponytail swinging in the cool breeze. "If you'll let me practice on you, you won't have to wait."

"That sounds promising," Lettie put in.

Joy clicked her tongue. "Lettie, please," she said with a smile.

Something shifted in Zach's chest, and he felt the urge to grab her to him again. To swing her up in his arms and feel her tremble against him.

Instead he flung his arms wide like Tom had done earlier. "Jingles, I'm at your disposal."

She clasped her hands. "You might regret that."

"Not a chance."

He was afraid of that very thing, but he wouldn't admit that. No. Right now he would take this as it came and leave his worries back on the Harris ranch.

Putting his arm over her shoulders, he turned her toward the bakery. "Now how about helping me choose something from the bakery?"

She nudged him with her hip. "If you want more peppermint, I'm your girl."

Zach just smiled. "Yep. You sure are."

And just like that, things changed between them. He wasn't sure of his future but he was certain of one thing. He wanted Joy to be a part of it somehow.

Chapter 10

Joy crossed her arms and surveyed the shelves in front of her. They stretched nearly to the ceiling of the huge arts and crafts store, and held so many different kinds of frames. She knew she could surely find something online but she wasn't able to touch them. To feel their scant weigh. They would hold something she hoped the recipients would treasure for years to come. For generations, even.

"I'd help you if you told me what you were looking for," Zach said.

He stood close behind her, and she couldn't resist leaning back against him as she looked skyward. He felt very solid behind her, his leather jacket smooth and his jeans rough. Giving herself a mental shake, she focused on the task at hand.

"I want something homey, yet not cheesy looking. Oval, I think. Or maybe square with an oval mat."

"Now you've lost me."

Joy laughed and faced him, losing her balance as she turned. He caught her arms and held her up. "Thanks."

"Any time."

She stared up at him and her breath caught. He was so beautiful. "Zach, I know you might think I'm kidding but I need you."

He arched a brow. "Do tell?"

"I want to practice on you." She winced. "I mean, practice my art."

He tilted his head toward the small shopping cart beside her. She'd found several packages of silhouette paper and about a dozen scissors. "Those are a lot of little scissors, Joy. I'm not sure what you want to practice, exactly."

She couldn't resist touching his face. "I wouldn't do anything to mar these chiseled cheeks, Cowboy. I promise to only cut paper."

"Deal."

Her hands clasped, she turned back to the shelves. Something caught her eye, the edge of a dark oval frame of coved molding. It was just about what she was looking for, matte black in finish to fit into just about any kind of décor.

"Can you lift that stack?" she asked, tugging at the frame.

"Sure."

Zach moved the frames piled on top of it and she slid the eight-inch tall oval out to examine it. "It's a little bigger than I was thinking, but if I cut an oval mat to fit inside it could work."

"If you say so."

She pictured it with a creamy mat, the beveled edge touched with gold. It would be understated, and let her subject stand out in bold relief. That familiar buzz, missing so long she could hardly recognize it, started in her chest and moved outward. This was it. It wasn't large and it wasn't world-changing, but it was art made personal by subject and recipient.

"Let's see how many of these they have, Zach. I'll order more but I need as many as they have by next week."

"Sure thing, Jingles." He waved over a guy in a blue smock who clearly worked there. "Hey, man. We need every one of these you have in stock."

The guy, an older man who probably made birdhouses and other stuff in his spare time, smiled. "Just that color?"

Zach looked at Joy for confirmation and she nodded.

"Yes, please. Matte black. I'll need some mats custom cut as well, and cardstock cut to fit."

She was all but bouncing in her Chuck Taylors as Zach put the boxes of supplies in the back of his truck. She wore his jacket now, since he'd handed it to her as he'd moved all of her boxes. It held his scent and felt very nice but it hadn't been necessary. The sweater she wore was sufficient for the late afternoon chill, and it wasn't like she'd bought out the store.

Good thing too, since she was on a limited budget.

"You look pretty happy there," he said as he closed the liftgate, laughter in his voice.

She nodded. "Oh, I am!" She began to remove his jacket when he held up a hand. "Keep it on, Jingles. You look cold. And hot."

His words filled her with heat, making his jacket completely unnecessary now. Dipping her head, she grabbed the empty cart and returned it to the front of the store. When she turned back he was standing there, his eyes dark and his hair windswept. Her fingers itched to dig through her new supplies and recreate that strong jaw. Those perfect lips.

"Ready?" he asked.

She nodded and when he opened her door she stepped up to sit inside. Reaching for the radio, she paused. "May I?"

"Sure thing."

She pushed the buttons until she found the local station. One of her favorite Christmas songs by the Carpenters filled the truck cab.

"Merry Christmas, Darling," she sang along, unable to resist the urge.

"Merry Christmas, Jingles," Zach said.

She shot him a glance, and saw a teasing glint in his eyes.

"I warned you, Cowboy. It's inevitable with me at this time of the year."

He shrugged. "I've liked what you've shown me about the holiday so far, Joy."

"What have I shown you?"

He winked, the expression playful and very sexy. "Mistletoe, for one. Then there was that delicious…peppermint mocha."

She suspected he was going to mention their kiss, kisses really, but she decided to play along. "That's only the beginning."

His hands tightened on the wheel, but she caught the curve of his cheek as he smiled. "Looking forward to it."

So was she. She might be setting herself up for a whole world of hurt, but there was one thing she knew for sure.

This was determined to make this a Christmas she'd remember for a long time.

***

"This isn't what I expected when you said you wanted to practice on me," Zach said.

They were in her little room, since she refused to come to

140

his again. She might have something there, since he was pretty sure if he ever got her close to his bed? He'd never let her out of it.

It didn't help that this room held her unique sweet and hot scent. It was clear that someone actually lived her once, since it wasn't furnished exactly like his guest room. The furniture was similar to his, but the pillows and other stuff like family pictures spoke of a personal space.

There were boxes stacked in one corner, but otherwise the room was neat. They had that in common, then. After his mother left, Zach gave himself the task of keeping the house picked up at least. He shook his head as he recalled all of the widows and divorcees who had volunteered their services cleaning the ranch house.

Joy clicked her tongue as she touched his chin. "Face the wall, Cowboy. And keep still."

He shifted on the small chair and tried to focus on a picture on the wall. It was a drawing of the inn, and judging by the carved wood frame, he could guess it was one Joy was pretty proud of.

"When did you draw that picture?" he asked.

She grew quiet and he risked another scolding by turning

to face her. There was an uncharacteristically sad expression on her face, her full lips turned down at the corners.

"I drew that for my father." She slowly drew in a breath, her shoulders tensing. "Right after we moved in."

"It's really good. How old were you?"

She fiddled with the tools spread out on the top of her desk. "Fifteen."

"You have real talent, Joy. That's pretty obvious, even to somebody like me."

She lifted her head and met his gaze. "Somebody like you?"

He shrugged. "Yep. I have no clue about art." He shifted on the chair. "For instance, I still don't know what you're doing."

That brought a small smile to her face. "What were you expecting, exactly? Did you want me to draw you like my French girls?"

He faced her fully. "Huh?"

She laughed now, a light sound. "Titanic reference, Zach. I'm not going to sketch you. I'm going to cut your silhouette."

His puzzlement must have shown, because she moved some stuff around on the top of her desk and held up what looked like a cardboard cutout.

"This, I'll admit, is a little bit rough." She turned it to face him and ran a finger down the edge. "This is you."

He narrowed his eyes on the board. "It's a guy."

"It's you. I cut it from memory, though."

Her admission made his chest ache. "You thought about me, Jingles?"

She put the cutout back on the desk and gazed at him, her big brown eyes dark. "Zach, I'm always thinking about you."

Damn. "I'm glad you have that going on," he admitted.

Her brows rose and she stroked a hand through her thick waves, pulling her hair over to one side. "Why, exactly?"

He turned to face her drawing of the inn again. "Because I have it going on, too." She sucked in a breath but he held his position. "Not cut me, or whatever you call it."

"Zach."

"Later, Jingles. After."

"Oh, fine. Sit still, then."

He wanted her to think about just what would happen after. He sure knew what he wanted to happen, and he would give her this time with her art if it made her happy. And then, if she let him, he would make her even happier.

"There!" she said after about five minutes.

Facing her, he gaped as he saw what she held in her hands. The thin black paper she'd bought, white on the other side, was cut and spread out on top of the desk. He stood and crossed to it, seeing two images facing each other. The curve of his chin, his Harris nose, even the suggestion of messy hair was captured in the precisely-cut silhouette.

"Damn, that's me," he murmured. "It's like you took a picture. Why are there two of them?"

"You have to place the sheets of paper together before cutting."

He turned to her, seeing the triumph lighting her face. "You're really good."

She bit that full lower lip and then gave a short nod. "Thank you."

He glanced at the silhouette again. "Except for one thing."

"What?" She stepped closer to him to study the paper. "What thing?"

"You gave me girly eyelashes, Jingles."

She laughed and turned back to him. "You have eyelashes, Zach." She brought a finger to his face, starting at his hairline and gently stroking his profile. "Long eyelashes that are

144

anything but girly. A straight, perfect nose." She touched his mouth. "Full lips." Her voice held a husky note. "I could look at your face all day."

His pulse pounded and he reached up to grasp her slender wrist. He could feel the flutter of her pulse too, and it ratcheted up the tension between them.

"Kiss me, Joy," he rasped.

She came up on her toes and brushed her delectable mouth against his. He wrapped his arms around her waist, pulling her tight against him. Her bed, a smaller version of the one in his room, was very tempting. Even the plump frou-frou pillows on it wouldn't get in his way. Putting his hands under her ass, he lifted her against him and tumbled her to the bed.

Her body arched beneath his, and he cupped one round breast in his hand. Her sweater was thin, and her lacy bra was a contrast that seemed to set her on fire. Good, because he sure as hell was burning up.

"Damn, Joy." He kissed her neck. Her throat. "You smell so damn sweet."

"Zach." She ran her hands over his back, holding him closer. "That feels so good."

He lifted her sweater, tickling her flat stomach as he urged it up and over her head. Lifting up on one elbow, he stared down at her breasts. Her bra was thin, and her nipples pink and pebbled beneath the fabric.

"So pretty." He teethed one nipple, drawing a low moan out of her. "Sweet here, too."

There was a front clasp, and he unfastened her bra in a second. The sight of her smooth pale skin and rosy nipples made him hard. He couldn't resist suckling her and she ran her fingers through his hair. She murmured something he couldn't catch, and then her hand cupped him through his jeans.

He groaned, his blood pounding low. She reached into his boxer briefs and stroked him. Her fingers were delicate and clever, and he wanted to return the favor. Her jeans were those thin, stretchy kind and he just pushed the waistband aside and touched her.

"Zach!" She arched again, moving against his questing fingers.

She was hot and wet, and he groaned low as he sent her close to the edge. She was working him too, with insistent strokes that had him bucking against her hand. Biting down on one of her breasts, he drove her to climax. He joined her in the next second, coming hard against her smooth belly.

Gasping in a shuddering breath, he brought his face to hers.

"Baby, that was…" He kissed her, her parted lips and her closed eyelids. "Christ, that was something."

She nodded, licking her lips as she opened her eyes. Her skin was flushed pink and her eyes sparkled. "That was amazing, Zach." Glancing down at where they both had their hands down each other's pants, she laughed. "We aren't even naked."

He regretfully withdrew his hand from her warmth and settled down beside her. "I haven't done that in years, Jingles."

"Mmm." She turned to face him, her smile wide. "What, exactly, haven't you done?"

"Heavy petting, Joy." He kissed her again because he could. She looked so satisfied, and a little fuzzy. "You okay?"

"Zach?" She took in a breath and gazed at him, her eyes clear and bright. "I feel fantastic."

Chapter 11

Joy didn't take her time in the shower on Friday morning. She'd slept like a rock after Zach left her room last night, and woke up a little later than usual. Drying herself briskly, she shook her head.

"Talk about not a creature was stirring," she murmured.

Humming to herself, she dried her hair and dressed. She wore another ridiculous holiday sweater today, this one red with a forest of Christmas trees knit into it. There were little shiny ball ornaments and tiny bows on the trees, but at least this sweater didn't light up.

Another pair of red-striped leggings, her black ballet flats, and she was ready for whatever her mother had in merry little mind. The photo op would begin this afternoon, and Joy wanted to prep the front parlor. Staging the photos was something she'd really enjoyed last year, and setting up the shots made it really simple for Tom to snap the pictures. She felt a tingle as she recalled just who would be in a lot of the pictures. Yummy Zach Harris, the Cypress Inn's resident St. Nick.

The jolly old elf met her in the lobby as she arrived downstairs.

"Good morning," Zach said, his voice all smoky and

intimate.

Joy flushed and took a quick look around. She didn't see her mother so she stepped very close to him and placed a hand on his broad chest. He wore another thin sweater, this one cream in color and nubby to the touch.

"Good morning," she whispered just before kissing him. She leaned back, pointing above their heads. "Mistletoe."

"Naughty, Jingles."

"Join me for coffee?"

"Can't. I'm headed out to Billy's place."

"The stables?"

"Yep." He shoved his hands in the pockets of his jeans. "He wants to partner with me."

"Zach, that's great."

"Could be, yeah."

She touched his arm. "I won't keep you then."

"It shouldn't take too long, but he texted me this morning about maybe going out to the Boathouse for lunch."

"Oh, the Boathouse is fun! Have you been there?"

"Nope. Maybe you and I can go there some night?"

She couldn't help but smile. "Sure. I'll see you later for the photo op."

"That's right. What time?

"Just be back here by four or so? That's when we'll need you."

"We." He smiled crookedly. "And what time will you need me, Joy?"

She pushed at him. "Don't start that. I might not be a redhead like Tom and Becky but I know I sure blush like one."

His smile widened. "I'll see you later, Jingles."

He started past her, headed for the door.

"And don't worry."

He turned back to her. "About what?"

"I'll have your costume ready."

He groaned and shook his head. "What did I get myself into?"

It was her turn to grin. "Christmas, Zach."

After snagging a cinnamon bun and dodging her mother, she poured herself a quick cup of coffee and went out onto the terrace. It was chilly this morning, and a sheen of dew glistened on the woven wicker chairs and cushions. She decided to sit in one of the Adirondack chairs on the east side of the terrace, ignoring the damp wood as she settled down and set her thick stoneware mug on the wide armrest. The main lakeshore across the expanse of sandy beach was touched by the morning sun. Thin clouds streaked across the sky and the cypress trees and live oaks seemed to reach toward them. She nibbled her roll, feeling a sense of inspiration begin to trickle through her. From the first time she'd seen this view, standing on the rise where the inn would be built with her father, she'd been caught.

It was so different from the east coast, with its crashing waves and busy boardwalks. This setting was quiet, most of the time. The kids ran all over the playgrounds just to the east of the inn's private beach, but she knew that at this hour they'd be at the community school ready to start their day. Come this afternoon their shouts and laughter would float in the inn's direction, but Joy wouldn't be outside to hear it. Nope. She would be working the parlor photo op, and she was actually looking forward to it.

She licked the icing off of her fingers and wrapped both hands around her mug. Last night had been eye-opening. She'd known Zach could kiss, and she wasn't surprised he knew his way around. Her reaction was what had stunned her. Most of her male classmates in her art classes had played for the other team, so she hadn't dated much as an undergrad. That much-lauded gap year of hers had been filled with mistakes and regrets. It was only by the grace of God and maybe a very busy guardian angel that she'd never gotten into any real trouble.

Odd jobs up in Orlando, more waitressing and working as a shop girl, had filled her time and put her in the path of egomaniacal metrosexual guys who cared more about themselves and their appearance than anything she might want. That extended to the few sexual encounters she'd had that year. In grad school she'd pretty much avoided dating of any kind, and last night with Zach made her wonder just what she'd been missing all this time.

He'd sure rung her jingle bells. That was for sure.

"Joy, here you are."

Joy jumped at the sound of her mother's voice. "Morning, Mom."

Her mother was in Mrs. Claus mode again, today's apron sporting tiny reindeer. "I'm counting on your talents today, Joy. That parlor has to look like the North Pole."

"Isn't that a little on the red nose, Mom?"

Her mother blinked, and then laughed. "Okay, okay. Maybe something more Norman Rockwell?"

Joy thought for a minute. "How about Norman Rockwell meets the Florida Highwaymen?"

Her mother knew the artists Joy was talking about, since one of the twenty-six African American artists' paintings hung over the mantle in the very parlor they would be using. The colors, the composition, really brought home the whole Old Florida vibe of the inn's common rooms. It might have been painted from the very view Joy faced this morning, or even the wilder far lakeshore out past Billy and Shannon's farm.

"I bow to your expertise, dear." Her mother clasped her hands. "I'm just so happy you're working here this year!"

Joy didn't bother to point out that she'd worked the photo op last year but, then again, Joy's heart hadn't been in it. The woman must have picked up on that. Karen Rollins was nobody's fool.

"Finish your coffee, Joy." She patted her upswept hair. "And then you can do your magic."

Joy watched openmouthed as her mother left her, basically, to her own devices. "Wow."

After draining her mug, she headed into the parlor. She figured she would pull a few pieces from the other rooms here on the first floor to keep that Old Florida feel, along with some of the antique holiday decorations on display elsewhere to bring in that classic Rockwell theme. She knew there were more in storage up in the attic. Maybe she'd ask Zach to help her later?

And maybe she'd taste more of his particular brand of holiday magic.

***

"I would say at least eight stalls," Zach told Billy, pacing off the plot of land his cousin had set aside for this new part of his project. "That should leave a large enough paddock."

Billy tapped on his phone as he took notes. "I found a few examples online, Zach." He thumbed through a few screens as he walked over to where Zach stood. "Tell me what you think."

Guilt stabbed at Zach, gone when he saw the guileless open expression on Billy's face. The guy was so damned decent, and he and Chase hadn't even given him a chance when he'd lost his parents.

"I think I was a dick."

Billy laughed. "Yeah, you were. I survived, man. Like I told your brother, that's all in the past."

Zach nodded, his throat thick. "Thanks." He looked through the photos on Billy's phone, seeing a few possibilities for what they were planning. "What do you think about horseback riding lessons, Billy? Do you think that would be a viable venture out here?"

Billy's mouth dropped open. "You're thinking about hanging around Cypress?"

Zach's gaze fell to the sandy ground beneath his boots. "I'm not sure, but I think getting a school up and running might be fun."

"Fun?"

At Billy's clearly doubtful tone, Zach faced him. "What?"

"You've never been one for fun, Zach. Not when you were a kid, and not in the years since."

Zach shoved his hands in his pockets. "I already admitted I was a dick."

"That's a whole different thing, cuz. I meant that when we were kids you were always so serious."

Zach shrugged. "Yep, I guess so. I played ball."

Billy grinned. "Yeah, you did. You were pretty good, man."

It surprised Zach that Billy had noticed. "You came to the games?"

Billy's cheeks reddened. "I might have caught a few games when you were on the mound."

Zach raised his brows. "I didn't know."

Billy reached out and placed a hand on Zach's shoulder.

"You might not have felt like it, but you and Chase? You were my family."

Zach's eyes pricked. "It sucked that your parents died, man."

"And it sucked that your mother left."

The two of them nodded, and then Billy pushed at his shoulder. "That's enough of that, I think."

Zach pulled in a breath. "You're a good guy, Billy."

Billy grinned. "That's why my lady loves me."

Zach went back to pacing off the paddock. "This size should work. Give the students plenty of room to learn how to care for the horses."

"And the stable should have a good-sized tack room," Billy said. "I don't think the goat's equipment will fit your and Chase's horse."

Zach laughed. "Not even close." He paused to look over at the large pen where the goats were running around. "The herd looks pretty happy."

"Yeah. A couple of the does are pregnant again."

Zach spied some of the fat little bodies looking a little more round in the middle. "You sound like a proud papa."

Billy nodded. "It's taken a while, but we found another

source not too far away in St. Cloud."

"Looks like you have several kids."

"Yeah, the tribe is growing."

"When do you think you'll be ready to open the petting zoo?"

"I'm not sure. Maybe after the holidays. Sometime in the spring."

"What about small horses, Billy? Little ones."

"What, for riding?"

"No, but pulling carts and stuff. Sometimes the big horses can spook little kids."

Billy crossed his arms. "And just how do you know what spooks little kids."

Zach slanted him a look. "Hey, I might have been born on a horse but that doesn't mean I was never afraid of them."

"Huh." Billy scratched his chin. "Yeah, the little guys might be a good addition. We can store their tack with in the stable, too."

"Seems to me like we need a bigger stable."

"I bow to your expertise, man."

"You have the degree, Billy."

"Maybe, but you're Wild Harry's firstborn son."

Zach straightened. "Challenge accepted."

Billy insisted on grabbing a burger at the Town Tavern with Zach for lunch, since they didn't have much time to head out to the Boathouse. Things seemed much smoother between them now, and Zach felt a little closer to his cousin by the time they were finished.

His phone buzzed in his pocket and he drew it out. He couldn't help smiling when he read the text.

Get your chestnuts over here, Cowboy.

"What's got you grinning, cuz?" Billy asked.

"The North Pole is calling."

Billy screwed up his face. "What?"

Zach took out a twenty dollar bill and put it on the table, and then came to his feet. "I have to go get fitted for a Santa suit, cuz."

Realization dawned on Billy's face and he grinned. "Nice."

Zach was still smiling as he parked his truck in the inn's lot. Shrugging out of his leather jacket, he walked through the lobby toward the stairs.

"Zach." The whisper caught him and he turned to find Joy peeking out of the parlor. "Oh, good."

He crossed over to her. "What's up, Jingles?" Her ponytail

was mussed and her sweater was rumpled.

"Having a rough day?" he asked.

She grabbed him by his waistband and tugged him into the room. He couldn't help but wrap his arms around her. "Easy there, Joy. It's the middle of the day, but I'm game if you are."

She gaped at him and he couldn't resist kissing her open mouth. After a second, she kissed him back. Memories of last night spiked his pulse and his body started to react.

Holding her away from him, he smiled at the cloudy expression on her face. "Now, what's so urgent?"

She brushed some loose waves back from her forehead and squared her shoulders. "Nothing, really. The photo op starts in less than two hours and I still have to arrange all of this stuff I had Tom drag down from the attic."

Zach looked around, seeing some old-fashioned wooden toys and several tufted and fringed footrests cluttering the room. "How can I help?"

The look of gratitude was almost as good as the sexy satisfied expression she'd worn last night. "Thanks, Zach."

She directed him on placement of the toys on the fireplace and hearth, replacing the glass knickknacks and other fussy stuff. He helped her move the tree closer to the flickering gas fireplace, happy the tree wasn't as real as it looked. She kept stepping back to take in the scene, her head tilted as she looked down at the digital camera in her hand.

"Okay, go sit in that chair," she said.

He made his way to the green velvet arm chair and sat. "Here okay?"

She looked down at the camera screen and nodded. "Yes, yes." Lifting her head, she beamed at him. "Zach, it's perfect."

He came to his feet. "I'm ready to suit up, Jingles."

Her eyes sparkled as she came closer. "Thanks again, Cowboy."

He loved putting that expression on her face, taking some of the worry out of those big brown eyes. Hell, he didn't even mind when she shoved the miles of red velvet at him and shooed him toward her brother.

"In here," Tom said, pulling him along. "Let's get you fat and jolly."

Casting a gaze at Joy over his shoulder, he caught her laughing at him. "Keep it up, Jingles. Payback's coming."

She winked and at that second he suspected he would go through just about anything to please her.

Chapter 12

Joy sent the last group off on their way, with candy canes and a small bag of her mother's best Christmas cookies as an added bonus. A welcome sort of exhaustion filled her. She'd made several appointments tomorrow morning for silhouettes too, and hoped to have a few pieces duplicated and ready to display at her booth next week.

She put a hand on her brother's shoulder. "Thanks, Tom."

"Sure thing, sis. I'm out." He loped out of the room. "See you, Mom. Zach."

Joy absently heard the others' responses and waved at her brother as she thumbed through the photos on the digital camera's small screen. The shots looked beautiful and the setting was just as she'd envisioned it. It was welcoming and nostalgic, and evoked the sensation of Christmas and everything it meant to her. She crossed to set the camera next to her laptop, almost hidden on a table in the corner.

"This went better than I'd expected," she said.

"Nonsense, dear." Her mother clicked her tongue. "You planned this perfectly, Joy. That's why it went so well."

Joy raised her head to face her mother, surprised. "Thanks Mom, but you're the one who set up the appointments."

She and Zach exchanged a look. Joy put her hands on her hips. "What did you two cook up?"

Her mother fiddled with one of her apron strings. "Oh, Zach and I had an idea. And we got Tom in on it."

Joy looked at Zach, whose brows raised beneath his thick white wig. "Tom took a couple of pictures of the setting with and without our Santa and sent them to the Sales Center."

Joy covered her mouth. Why hadn't she thought of that? "That's a great idea! We'll have to send some over to the bakery and coffee shop. Maybe the market, too."

Zach chuckled, but the sound was nothing like St. Nick might make. Still, she smiled.

"You were great today, Zach."

He had been fantastic, too. And very patient. Some of the families didn't want their photo with Santa, and he was such a good sport about popping up and down out of his grand chair.

He made a pretty fine Santa. That was for sure. Tom had stuffed him with a few pillows, but his shoulders still looked pretty wide in comparison to his round belly. And those eyes? Twinkling at her from beneath that snowy white wig, they were the eyes of a saint and a sinner at the same time.

"Joy, that was amazing!" Her mother clapped and

curtseyed to Zach. "Well done, Santa."

Zach shot her a wink and smiled in Joy's direction. "Just doing what I was told, ma'am."

"Then go and get comfortable. I think you've earned the late dinner Joy ordered."

"Dinner?" he asked.

"I ordered pizza from the tavern," Joy said.

"And I'll let you two relax then. Good night!"

Zach nodded and pushed the hat and wig off of his head, tugging down on his beard to slip that off too. "I think I should go easy on the pizza," he joked, his hands on his plump belly.

She watched as he withdrew the pillows and ran a hand through his tousled hair. He looked so hot right now, with the T-shirt he wore clinging to his very impressive chest and the big Santa coat hanging on either side of his narrow waist. Unable to resist, she moved closer and placed her hands on his velvet-covered shoulders.

"I've been a very good girl," she said with a smile.

Heat flared in his eyes. "Want me to fill your stocking?"

His words were silly and sexy, and just perfect for the moment. He bent his head to hers and kissed her, and she ran a hand down over his ridged abdomen.

He growled a little, the sound stroking over her. "What are you thinking, baby?"

He'd called her that before, and it sounded pretty darn good.

"How about we share that pizza in your room, Zach?"

"That's the best idea I've heard today."

She helped him out of the rest of the costume, setting it aside for tomorrow's photo shoot. "Why don't you head on up and I'll bring the pizza when it comes?"

He grasped the back of her neck, drawing her close for a lingering kiss. "Sounds good."

She watched him go, and then splayed her hand over her chest. Her heart raced beneath her palm and she caught her breath. Taking the camera and laptop up to her room, she changed out of her elf costume and dressed for dinner with Zach. In his room.

There would be more fooling around tonight. She'd seen the flare in his blue eyes. She slipped on a pair of yoga pants, some fluffy socks and a long-sleeve T bearing the black and gold UCF Knights logo. The armor-plated guy was armed with a sword which crossed right over her heart. It wasn't much protection. Not against what she was starting to feel for Zach.

Was she ready for this kind of, she guessed it was a relationship? They were friends. Almost from the first time she'd talked to him at Thanksgiving she'd felt a connection. He seemed to like hanging around with her too, but what did she know?

"Friends with benefits, then," she said to herself.

Ick. She'd never had one of those. He'd said he wasn't seeing anybody else, but would that change? Was she in any position to say otherwise?

Before she could talk herself out of going up to his room, she headed down to the lobby just as the front door bell rang. She just wouldn't think about anything but hanging out with her friend. Her very hot friend who'd given her an orgasm last night, but still.

She paid the pizza guy and padded up the stairs to Zach's room. Her fist held up to his door, she took a breath and knocked lightly. He opened the door wide, a smile on his face

"Jingles."

She laughed, shaking her head. "I'm not wearing any bells right now, Zach."

He took the pizza box and small bag of napkins and stuff from her and closed the door behind her. "Doesn't mean I won't ring 'em later."

She crossed to the opened French doors leading to his balcony. The sky was an inky indigo, the stars winking brightly. She knew the reason was the dark-sky compliant lights required in Cypress Corners. The special lights kept migrating birds from getting confused and misdirected. Still, the sight of those stars with differing levels of brightness? Just gorgeous.

She felt his hands on her shoulders. "Pretty, huh?" he asked, his chin on the top of her head. "I know it's chilly, but I was a little overheated after wearing that suit."

Crossing her arms, she nodded. "It's so pretty. I can almost imagine what Van Gogh felt, looking at those stars."

He turned her to face him and kissed her lightly. "Just don't go cutting anything off." He shut the doors. "Besides, I'm hungry."

He'd set the pizza on the small table near the fireplace, which was giving off a nice amount of heat. Not that she needed it. Just being so close to him nearly set her on fire.

"Water okay?" he asked, pulling two bottles out of the fridge.

"Water's fine." She took a bottle and sat across from him as he dug into the pepperoni pizza. "That really was great today,

Zach. I can't thank you enough."

He chewed and nodded. "Everybody loved you, Joy. They did just what you told them."

"Hmm. I must have used my teacher voice."

He raised his brows. "Maybe I'll let you tell me what to do later."

She shook her head and took a piece of pizza for herself, setting it on the lid of the opened box. "You might have started out all strong and silent, but you're sure a different guy now."

"Only when I'm around you," he said simply.

His statement made her heart give a thump. Pulling a slice of pepperoni free of her slice, she mulled that little piece of information as she chewed.

"Why is that, do you think?" she had to know.

He finished chewing and wiped his mouth with a napkin. "I like being around you." He winked. "You're such a joy to be with."

She kept her eyes down, feigning acute interest in her slice of pizza. "Are we friends?"

***

Zach thought about her question for a hot second. "I like to think so." He stroked his fingers over the back of her hand.

"Don't you?"

She met his gaze, her eyes bright and warm. "Yes."

He flashed her a smile, which he realized was becoming a frequent occurrence when he was around her, and went back to eating. She did likewise, finally leaning back in her chair.

"That was good," she said, drinking the last of her water.

"Yep, they make a good pizza." He closed the now-empty pizza box. "You know, I never realized just how much they have out here."

"What do you mean?"

"The restaurants and the bakery. The coffee shop."

"You've been out here to visit Chase and Billy before Thanksgiving, haven't you?"

He nodded. "Sure, but I didn't hang around the town square."

"I love it," she said. "It's what made me fall in love with Cypress back then." She lifted her chin toward the balcony again. "That, and the view."

He saw a wistfulness he'd caught before, like when the artist in her was taking over. It was sexy as hell, and when she bit that full lower lip? *Damn.*

"Joy."

She looked back at him, her brow furrowed. "What?" She grabbed her napkin and wiped it over her cheek, her chin. "Do I have something on my face?"

He shook his head and reached for her hand to still her. "Nah, baby. I'm just staring at that gorgeous face of yours."

He might not have Chase or Billy's charm, but he seemed to know what to say and do around Joy. She lit up like a, okay like a Christmas tree, and he couldn't wait to kiss her again.

She seemed to be thinking the same thing, because she got up and bridged the short distance between them to sit on his lap. It was nothing like the countless times somebody had sat on his lap today. That was for damn sure. This was his brunette, his Joy, and he loved the way she felt so close to him.

"Thank you again for all of your help today," she said. "And agreeing to do this through the season? My mother's beside herself."

He shook his head, his hands on her narrow waist. "I'm not doing it for your mother, Joy."

"No?"

He shook his head. "I'm doing it for you."

She kissed him and he closed his eyes, coming to his feet to hold her close. Her smooth, tight pants hugged her just right and he palmed her ass. She made a soft, purring sound as she came in full contact with his dick. His jeans were really tight now, but he still held her close as he ramped up the tension between them.

No other woman had ever made him feel so…hungry. She tasted like the pizza they'd shared, but also like the hot peppermint flavor he figured he'd always associate with only her. He pushed her shirt up and over her head, letting her hair fall back over her smooth back. Cupping her breasts through her lacy bra, he caught her moan against his mouth.

"Zach, please," she breathed.

"I will, baby." He kissed her throat. "I promise."

He urged her over to his bed, placing her on the edge while he tore off his shirt. It felt hot as hell in his room at this second, plus he wanted to feel her hands all over him. She seemed to read his mind, and came up on her knees as she ran her hands over his chest. She'd done that downstairs in the parlor, put those graceful fingers on his belly until he'd groaned. Now, with nothing between her touch and his skin, it set him on fire.

Bending his head, he kissed her again as her fingers got to work on his button fly. Straightening a little, he watched as she worked. She had good hands, his girl. It must come from being an artist, but right now he didn't care why her fingers were so nimble. Almost before he was aware of it, she had his cock out of his briefs and was stroking him like she had last night. Her touch was perfect. Slow and deep, and it made him ache.

"Damn, Joy." She glanced up at him and he caught her heated gaze with his. "Do you know what you do to me?"

She licked her lips and nodded. "And I know what I'm going to do to you."

Bringing her rosy mouth to his flesh, she began to lick and kiss him. Pushing his fingers through her thick chestnut waves, he cradled her head as she drove him out of his mind. Every brush of her tongue, every nip of her teeth, sent him galloping toward release. He was going to come and come hard, and he couldn't stop it any more than he could keep the stars from shining in that pretty Cypress sky.

"Ah, baby." His body gave a kick as his climax began. "Joy."

He squeezed his eyes shut and came, losing himself in her. When he came to his senses, he looked down to find her sitting back on her heels. In his bed. She'd just blown his mind and she was sitting there like the cutest, sexiest thing he'd ever seen.

"Please with yourself, Jingles?"

She laughed, her eyes dancing. "Interesting choice of words, Cowboy."

He tucked himself back into his briefs and kicked off his jeans. She crab-walked back on the bed, a big smile on her face as her eyes went wide.

"What are you doing?" she teased.

"Ah, Jingles." He stretched out over her until every part of him touched her. "I'm gonna fill your stocking."

Chapter 13

Joy didn't know exactly what he meant, but his gorgeous eyes were dark on hers. As dark as that indigo sky framed by the French doors.

"You're the sexiest thing, Jingles." He kissed her neck and then between her breasts. "I don't think I'll ever get enough of you."

His words weren't perfect, like some romance novel hero, but they were hot and felt as honest and straightforward as Zach himself. His big hands ran all over her as he began to teeth her nipples through the lace. Her bra was gone a minute later and he suckled one breast and then the other, until she was panting.

"Oh, my." It was dumb, but just about the only thing she could manage to say. "Zach."

He tugged her pants down her legs, taking her panties with them. Kissing her belly, he dipped his tongue in her navel. It tickled, but the site of his dark head moving lower still was anything but funny. Heat flushed to her center, and then he was there. His lips and tongue caressing her until she could only close her eyes and grab on to the bed covers beneath her.

"You're so hot, baby." He kissed her inner thigh, sliding a finger into her. "Hot and sweet."

He ran the rough edge of his tongue over her swollen nub, wringing a cry out of her. She was vaguely thankful that her mother's room was two floors away. Heck, she knew how well the inn was built. She bet she could scream to her heart's content and no one would hear her.

"Zach, please," she said for what felt like the hundredth time. "Oh. Oh!"

He lifted his head and she nearly screamed in frustration.

"Look at me, baby."

She swallowed and managed to look down at him. Oh, her heart raced at the passion etched on his handsome face. His pupils were dark and his lips, those incredibly mobile lips, parted before he slid her a slow smile.

"Zach," she said again.

"Tell me what you want, Joy."

She swallowed again. "Make me come."

He winked, actually winked, and returned to his task. Her blood was pounding now, her entire body strung tight as he drove her unerringly toward release. She cried out, his name and a few other things she couldn't really recall, and came.

Before she'd stopped trembling he was right there next to her, his lips on her throat as he buried his face in her neck.

"You're amazing, baby." He kissed her slowly now, his fingers still stroking over her tender flesh. "Do you remember what you said?"

She opened her eyes, finding his twinkling at her. "Do I want to know?"

He let out a breath and propped himself up on one elbow. "Pretty naught for an elf, if you ask me."

She covered her face with one hand. "I'm sorry."

He took her hand, lowering it as he shook his head at her. "I don't think I've ever heard you use those particular four-letter words before. And I think there was something about my tongue."

"Okay, fine." She found a smile for him but it took a lot of energy. "You made me lose control, Cowboy. Not all of us can reach that particular peak and keep their wits."

He gaped at her. "Are you kidding me? I nearly fell over from what you did to me earlier."

She came up on her elbows now, not caring in the least that she was naked. "Seriously?"

He traced one finger over her cheek, giving a slow nod. "Jingles, that was the best I'd felt in a long time."

Picking up the coverlet at the end of the bed, he drew it up over the both of them. She turned slightly, and he tucked her up against the front of him. They cuddled, as amazing as that should be. Her big strong cowboy was a cuddler. Who knew?

"So, friends?" he asked, gently biting her earlobe.

"Friends." She fought to keep her tone light. "With benefits."

His arm tightened and she turned to see a frown marring the perfection of his face. "No, Joy. This isn't just because you and I happen to be living under the same roof."

Wriggling, she faced him fully. "Why, then?"

"I like you." He rolled his eyes. "That's lame. I sound like I'm in fourth grade."

She ran her gaze over his sculpted chest, seeing the light dusting of golden hairs, and shook her head. "No. I've been in fourth grade. Heck, I've taught fourth grade."

That made him smile. "Okay, teach. I don't just fall into bed with somebody because they're convenient. Not anymore."

She wanted to believe him. "You said we're friends."

"We are. And I sure as hell wouldn't use a friend that way." His eyes crinkled at the corners. "I can honestly say I've never fooled around with a friend before."

"So, not friends with benefits?" She had to know for sure,

no matter how silly she sounded. "Then, what are we?"

He looked down, lightly stroking her arm until he covered her hand with his. "How about we just say we're dating?"

"Dating?" She sat up, holding the coverlet over her breasts. "I guess we can say that."

She wasn't going to label them boyfriend and girlfriend, and he didn't seem inclined to do so either. Nibbling her lip, she decided to go all in with another prickly question.

"Are we dating anyone else?" she asked.

"Nope."

His answer was short and very sweet. Sliding back down next to him, she hummed in contentment.

"Good," she said.

He squeezed her for a beat, and then kissed her again.

***

Saturday morning, Zach sat back with his cinnamon roll and mug of coffee as he watched as Joy worked her magic. Her tiny scissors flew and the concentration on her beautiful face was a piece of art all on its own. She was quick, and her pieces were amazing when she finished. Without exception her cutouts were somehow the perfect image of her subjects, and the frames he'd helped her get were just right for the silhouette portraits.

He recognized a few of the families from the photo op the day before, but he couldn't exactly remind them of that. Every so often one of the mothers or fathers would do a doubletake, and Zach just kept his face fixed in a polite expression. He wasn't going to be the one to shatter their kids' illusions of Santa Claus. Nope. He was content to drink his coffee. Enjoy his roll. And watch the remarkable woman who had slept in his arms last night.

He hadn't pushed for more than they'd already shared. He'd never been that type of guy, but he'd never had to be. With Joy it was different, though. She was different. He would take his cues from her and dance to her Christmas carols if she asked him. He smiled into his coffee mug. Maybe not dance exactly, but he would let her take the reins on their relationship.

She'd seemed reluctant to talk about that subject after their awkward boyfriend/girlfriend discussion. They were friends who were dating. That was a first for him. He figured if he could get past Christmas without screwing things up, he might actually have a chance at a Happy New Year.

"There! What do you think?" Joy said to her latest little subject.

It was something she'd said to just about every kid this

morning, and just about every kid reacted the same way. Excitement and amazement, while their parents or grownups oohed and aahed over the framed artwork. Every so often she held one up for him to see, a wide smile of accomplishment on her face. And every so often a punch of something other than lust hit him square in the gut.

"Zach dear, there is still food left in the dining room," Joy's mother said as she peered into the parlor.

"I'm still full from my first run through the food line, Mrs. Rollins." He held up the last bite of his cinnamon roll before popping it into his mouth. "Always room for these, though."

Mrs. Rollins laughed and walked over to where the duplicate silhouettes were matted and awaiting frames. "Oh, Joy! These are wonderful!"

"Thanks, I love them too," Joy said.

Mrs. Rollins tucked her hands behind her back as she leaned over them as if afraid to touch. Zach could relate. The artwork was only paper, as amazing as that was, but they looked fragile. Like a delicate kind of carving or something.

"Just so...I don't know what to say." She straightened. "You're going to sell a ton of these this weekend!"

"I sure hope so. I'm not going to get rich, but I'd like to

start making my own way."

Zach heard something in Joy's voice, that wistfulness he'd caught the first night they'd gone out. Her mother placed a hand on Joy's shoulder, and the look they shared made Zach feel out of place. His chest grew tight and hot.

Mrs. Rollins kissed her daughter's cheek, smiled at Zach, and left the parlor.

"I'm sorry." Joy swiped at her eyes, shrugging. "I didn't realize how much it meant to me."

"What?" He stood and crossed to her, brushing a thick lock of her hair behind her ear. "Your art?"

"No." Her eyes shone. "My mom's approval."

"You deserve nothing less, Jingles." He wanted to kiss her, to hold her, but he had things to do and so did she.

"I'll leave you to this, Joy."

"You're headed out to Billy's?"

He nodded. "We have some details to go over. I want to take you to dinner, though. Maybe that Boathouse you told me about?"

She nodded, lifting up on her toes to kiss him. It was brief, just a touch of her lips, but it eased the tightness in his chest. "And then you're on duty again."

"Yep, I know." He winked. "See you later, Jingles."

A couple of hours later, he drove back from Billy's place. There was a whole lot of info written in his spiral notebook. He knew it might be strange, but it seemed like he could always read his own handwriting better than anyone else's or any printed words. If people looked at him like he was weird for writing things with an actual pen, he didn't give a shit. He didn't want to miss anything he and Billy had talked about. This was about business, but it was also about family.

Shannon had wanted to give him breakfast, but he'd passed. Chase and Carrie were there too, of course. And that adorable little carrottop, Caitlyn. The baby looked a little like her mother but she had a whole lot of Harris in her. It was weird to think that he had a tie to his niece, but it was a nice kind of weird.

It was also weird that everybody seemed to know he and Joy were dating. It was the first thing Shannon had asked when she'd opened the farmhouse door, for God's sake. He'd been warned about the fishbowl, hadn't he? Joy's brother had clarified it and Lettie's sharp gaze on him as he got out of his truck in front of the coffee shop now seemed to set it in concrete.

"Zachary Harris." She wrapped her thick sweater around

herself and grinned. "Happy Sunday morning to you."

He dipped his head. "Good morning, ma'am."

She lost her smile and her eyes went round. "Zach, can I talk to you for a moment?"

The older woman almost looked worried about something. That wasn't what he'd ever seen on her face. Cunning, yep. Nosy as all get out, sure. Sweet-tempered though, which made the furrow he spied underneath her big straw hat seem very unusual.

"What's wrong, Lettie?"

Her smile returned. "Why, nothing dear boy! I just wanted to speak to you."

"Is this about Joy?"

Now she smiled. "You and that sweet girl are an item, then? I knew it."

Zach wasn't going to get into this with her, not out here in the busy town square. A few people walking past smiled and waved, and he nodded in return before facing Lettie again.

"I was just going to grab a couple of peppermint mochas, Lettie. Can whatever this is wait a minute?"

She started to shake her head, and then she sighed. "No, I guess there's nothing for it now."

182

"What do you mean?" he asked.

Her gaze held a touch of concern, but he was damned if he knew why. "I'm sorry, Zachary."

"Sorry for what?"

"Zachary," a woman said from behind him.

His stomach clenched. *No. It couldn't be.* Turning, he faced a woman he hadn't laid eyes on in over twenty years. Her eyes were like his, that dark blue he faced in the mirror every day since she'd left. Her hair was still dark and pulled back with a wide headband. She looked older. Smaller than he remembered. But there was no mistaking it. It was Helen Harris. His mother.

He took a breath and tried to slow his racing heart. Her eyes stared into his, the emotion behind them beyond what he could figure out at this second.

"Hello, son," she said.

Without another word to her or to Lettie, he turned on his heel and stalked back to his truck.

Chapter 14

Joy directed the kids on either side of the big chair where Zach sat. He was quiet today, but that wasn't so unusual. No, he seemed different somehow. She hadn't seen him after he'd met with Billy. Maybe something happened to strain the fragile relationship between him and his cousin.

"Look over here, Santa," she called, shooting him a smile.

He shifted and did as she'd asked, and the photo would be almost as good as any taken yesterday. If somebody didn't compare them and notice the decided lack of spark in St. Nick's eyes in today's, however.

She'd sat at the desk in her room after he'd left this morning, poring over today's silhouettes. She'd only had a few minutes to finish framing the duplicates before she'd had to suit up like an elf and get downstairs to the parlor for today's photo op. The bells on her skirts jingled as she moved and directed both the subjects and her brother Tom.

"I got it, sis," he said with a short laugh. "It's not my first rodeo. Get it, Santa?"

Santa gave Tom a small smile, gone in a second. The afternoon was pretty successful, in her opinion anyway. By the time the last group left, candy canes and Christmas cookies held in the children's hands, she was ready to ask Zach just what the heck was wrong.

"I'm taking off, Joy," Tom said, handing the camera over to her. "See you, Santa."

Zach waved a hand, but she could see that his mouth was dipped down at the corners. He was a very un-jolly St. Nick at the moment. After she was sure there weren't any other kids in the lobby, she shut the parlor doors and faced him.

"Zach, what's wrong?"

He opened his mouth to protest, and then hung his head. "I'm sorry, Joy. I was a dud today."

As he removed the hat, wig and beard, she could see how torn up he was about whatever was going on. His cheeks were ashen, and her heart rose in her throat.

"Oh, what happened?" She crossed over to him, setting a hand on his cheek. "You look, well you always look great, but right now you look so sad."

His brows rose. "Sad? Yep, maybe. Pissed off? Definitely."

She kissed him, she couldn't not kiss him at the moment, and straightened. "Let's go grab a beer at the tavern."

He shook his head as he shrugged out of the velvet Santa

coat. "No. I don't want to go anywhere near the town square."

"What happened between you and Billy?"

"What? Nothing, Jingles. Billy and me, we're fine. Great, even. It was later." He pushed out a breath, ending on a soft groan. "Sorry to be a downer."

She bit back any cheery platitudes she might have given him if he hadn't looked so seriously downhearted.

"Let's go to the Boathouse then. Not many Cypress folks go there."

"Cypress folks." He brushed his hair back from his forehead. "I guess that's good."

"I'll get changed and we can go?"

He reached for her, pulling her close. "Thanks, baby."

His kiss was soft and sweet, and her heart nearly crumbled. When he let her go she packed up her laptop and camera and hurried upstairs.

That look of preoccupation was still on his face when she joined him in the lobby. She'd changed into a pair of jeans and a sweater, and wrapped a soft scarf around her neck. He'd changed too, and now wore a sexy Henley under his leather jacket.

She smiled up at him. "I like this look, but I think I prefer you in red velvet."

He growled playfully at her, a light coming into his eyes at last. "And I think I want to see you in those striped tights, Jingles."

Thankful for her mother's penchant for hanging mistletoe, she used it for the opportunity it gave her. Reaching up, she placed her hands on his face and kissed him. He didn't even hesitate, returning her kiss deeply. She might not know exactly what they were, but they were dating. Dating each other and no one else, so she was going to kiss him any time she wanted to.

Slowly coming back down on her heels, she sighed. "Ready?"

Now that light in his eyes began to twinkle. "Baby, that's a loaded question."

"Save that for later, Cowboy."

He took her hand, which was a first, and tugged her alongside of him as they headed out to his truck. "There'll be a later, Joy? After what I pulled today?"

"What, exactly, did you pull?"

He shrugged one of those broad shoulders. "I was kind of a dick, Jingles. I could have ruined today's shoot."

"Never in a million years, Zach. You might not have been you're usual teasing self, but you were still very good."

He held the passenger door open. "Wait, I'm usually a tease?"

Her cheeks flushed and stepped up and in. "Not touching that at the moment, but you were a jolly Santa yesterday. Today you were more of a noir kind of guy."

"Noir." He walked around and got in behind the wheel. "I guess that's art talk?"

She shook her head. "Sort of. Noir, like the moody darkly-lit films of the forties and fifties. Noir is French for black."

"Huh." He started the truck and pulled out of the lot. "I'm learning a lot from you, Joy."

She winced. "Sorry, but I'm kind of a dork."

"You're not." He ran his gaze over her outfit of dark jeans and thin sage sweater. "You're kind of adorable, and just what I need."

He seemed as surprised by his words as she was, but neither of them said a thing to correct it. If she were being completely honest, she loved that he needed her. She sure was starting to need him, and more than just his kisses.

After they drove for about ten minutes she pointed out a turn-off to the right. They followed a winding road which led through the woody growth toward what looked like little more than a sprawling shack by the lakeside.

The Boathouse was located around the bend from the main lakeshore, but mostly folks who boated in from the inlets to the north frequented the place. It boasted a lone dock to the rear with a few small boats tethered to it. It was the definition of rustic, and looked like something out of an old painting. Muted colors, faded boards and a rusted tin roof.

"Tin roof…rusted," she sang, a line from one of her favorite eighties songs.

He chuckled as he parked the truck beside a wooden light post. "I think that's country slang for being pregnant."

She laughed. "I'd heard that, yes. Still a great line."

"I'll give you that one."

Lights shone inside the shack and she could hear music on the chilled air as they stepped out of the truck. Country-style Christmas carols. She smirked at Zach and he just shook his head. He seemed a little bit looser now, and she silently vowed to keep doing whatever she was doing that was bringing him out of that funk.

***

Zach walked behind Joy over the sandy, weed-choked parking lot to the restaurant. That was no hardship. Her jeans hugged her perfect curves and that sight, and her sweetness, was going a long way to rid him of the sick feeling he'd had since seeing his mother in the town square.

He wasn't surprised to find the Boathouse was loud and crowded and filled with wooden picnic tables. It felt like it could be any place in the country, frequented by locals and never drawing any of the tourists who only thought of the Mouse when thinking about Central Florida.

The hostess showed them to a table near the wide screened windows and she sat on the bench across from Zach.

It felt like they were still outside; the chirps and croaks of everything that lived in the woods were muted as well this time of year, and the air was cool and crisp through the screened windows. A server, an older woman who looked like she'd been born a waitress, stopped by the table and handed each of them a menu.

"Now this is more like it," he said as he viewed their offerings. "Catfish. Turnip greens. Gator tail. A small but great list of local and domestic beers." He smiled at her. "Good idea, Jingles. I've got to bring Chase and Billy out here."

"My dad used to love this place."

He caught that wistfulness, and set the menu down. "Do

you get here much?"

She shook her head. "Nope. My mother was pretty busy with the inn after he died, and now it's pretty much her whole life."

"But not yours?"

"Not complete, no. It's not Becky's or Tom's either, no matter how hard my mother tries."

"You'll work for her, though."

"In a heartbeat, Zach. It's not a tough thing. My mom's a good woman, and I see my dad around every corner."

The server came back and Zach ordered everything that caught his eye. She and Joy exchanged a look and he shrugged.

"Everything looks good." He handed the server the menu. "Don't worry, Jingles. I'll share."

He ordered a couple of beers too, and sat back. Taking in a big breath, he slowly let it out. "This was a great idea, baby. Thanks."

She studied him for a minute, concern in her gaze. Brenda Lee rocked around the Christmas tree to fill the quiet that settled over their table. It wasn't an uncomfortable silence, and as their beers came and they dug into some pretty spectacular food he realized he'd never just spent time with a woman before her.

Maybe he was growing up. It sure beat the shit out of being the lost little boy he'd felt like when he'd seen his mother.

As they finished their beers, her second and his third, she folded her arms on the scarred had-once-been-painted-green picnic table. That easy quiet was over. He knew it in his gut.

"Are you going to tell me what happened?" she asked.

He started to argue, unable to even think of a lie to feed her. "Nothing happened, Joy. Nothing that matters."

"You always struck me as a straight-shooter, Zach. Don't start hiding stuff now."

He glanced around the restaurant, seeing no one he recognized, and set his bottle down. "I saw my mother today."

Joy's eyes widened and her mouth dropped open. "Oh, Zach. Where? When?" She held up a hand. "Never mind the when. It must have happened while you were out a Billy's."

"Just after, actually. Outside the coffee shop."

She reached across the table and took his hand, her fingers curling around his fist. "I'm so sorry."

"What's the weirdest thing is that Lettie woman? I think she knew."

Joy shook her head. "She knows everything, that woman. It wouldn't surprise me in the least."

"She tried to warn me off, kind of."

"How does she know your mother?"

"I have no idea and I didn't stick around to find out." He heard the bitterness in his voice, and turned his hand to grasp hers. "I couldn't talk to her. I just couldn't."

"That's natural, I would think."

"No, Joy." Anger flared through him, reminding himself how pissed he'd been since that little run-in. "I acted like a pussy. Like a scared little boy who tucked tail and got the hell out of there."

"Whoa, Zach. You haven't seen her in what, twenty years?"

"More," he bit out.

"What do you think you should have said to her? What do you think you should have done? Maybe you should have bought her a cup of coffee?"

His anger lowered to a simmer as he looked into her toffee brown eyes. "Nah."

The server came back to the table. "You two need anything else?"

"Just the check, please." He looked over at Joy. "If that's okay, Joy?"

Joy nodded, her fingers stroking over his arm now. The server left and he stared down at their clasped hands. He needed her. Just her. He needed to hold Joy at the moment, and in the privacy of his room.

They were quiet once again on the ride back to the inn. The place was quiet too, and they made their way up to his room. It was like she knew what he needed, and at this second he wasn't going to do any heavy thinking to figure out why. She was his Joy. His brunette. His Jingles.

His jacket and her thick nubby scarf shared the leather ottoman not far from the fireplace. He started a fire with the flick of a switch, but he crossed to the balcony and opened the doors wide. That now-familiar nightscape met his gaze, and he stared up at the stars.

He thought about the kid he'd been when his mother left, and for a split-second he considered making a wish on one of those stars. What would he wish for, exactly? A do-over? That his mother had never left them? Right now it felt like he was all out of wishes.

Joy stepped behind him, wrapping her arms around his waist and resting her cheek against his back. He was seized with the idea that he'd wished for her.

"Tell me," she urged softly.

Sucking in a deep breath of crisp, fresh air, he tried to gather his thoughts about the woman. He gripped the fancy wrought-iron railing and stared out at the dark trees dripping moss toward the glistening lake. Joy was right about this view. It was almost as pretty as she was.

"She was gone when Chase and I came home from school," he said.

Joy came around to his side, covering his hand with one of hers again. "How old were you again?"

"I was ten. Chase was eight."

"And you had no idea?" She shook her head. "Of course you didn't. You were a kid."

"I knew my mother and father didn't have a regular relationship, Joy. At least not one like the parents of some of my friends from little league."

"Did they fight?"

"Hell no, they didn't fight. They didn't even talk."

"Yikes."

He saw her shiver and he drew her into his arms, running his hands over her back as he breathed in her scent. "My dad changed after that. If he was cold before, he was downright frozen from then on."

"I just don't get it."

"No, you wouldn't. You have a mother who loves you. A dad you remember so well that you can't keep the light from your eyes when you talk about him."

She pulled back, staring up at him for a long minute. "You see a lot, Cowboy."

He touched her smooth cheek, running his thumb over her lower lip. "I see a woman who cares, Joy. About everybody, sure. But also about me."

"I do," she whispered.

"Call me conceited, but at the moment that's all I want to think about right now." He cupped her face, bringing his lips to hers. "You and me, Jingles. And how we care about each other."

She pressed against him, her eyes darker than the night sky now and more beautiful than the stars above them.

"Show me, Zach." Her mouth brushed against his, the kiss feather-light. "Show me how much you care?"

He placed his hands under her ass and lifted her in his arms. "Gladly."

Chapter 15

Joy couldn't stop looking up at Zach as he carried her into his room. He set her on the edge of the bed, like he had last night, and crossed back to the balcony to close the doors. She kicked off her heels and slid up on the bed, sitting cross-legged. Her heart hammered in her chest and she wiped her palms over her thighs.

He pushed a couple of buttons on the wall near the door and lowered the lights. Now the room was lit by firelight and ambient lighting up by the ceiling. His guest room was one of the prettiest in the inn, which she'd known when her mother had told her to show him to it when he'd first moved in. It was hard for her to believe that had been just a week ago.

He stepped over to the bed and pulled his shirt up over his head. "You ready, Jingles?"

She swallowed and nodded, her skin flushed. He was beautifully built, and as an artist and as a woman she could appreciate the sculpted lines of his body. She'd seen him last night, of course. But not standing here in front of her, so warm and real. And hers, if she gave in to the wish she'd made standing out on his balcony.

He bent down and placed his hands on either side of her

hips. His eyes were dark as he urged her to stretch out beneath him, soon all but covering her with his body.

"You have on way too many clothes, Joy."

She agreed, and lifted her hips as he drew her jeans down her legs. When he came up to push off her sweater, she raised her arms over her head and then wrapped them around his neck. This was like last night, but so much more. A small doubt niggled at the back of her mind, warning her against getting too close too fast. She stubbornly willed it to shut the heck up, because this was Zach. The guy who'd been abandoned by his mother and was reconnecting with his family. He was the guy who sparked her in more ways than one.

"Ah, Jingles." His lips ran over her skin, trailing down to her breasts to tease her. "So sweet."

She hummed with pleasure as he moved lower, making her ache for more of him.

"Please, Zach."

He came up to kiss her, and then stood to drop his jeans. Reaching into his pocket, he withdrew a condom packet. She was so hot now, as lit as the flames behind the glass fireplace screen. Every bit of her body wanted his. Wanted him.

"Are you sure, baby?" He paused, his hands on the

waistband of his boxer briefs. "Is this too much, too soon?"

She shook her head and came up on her knees, taking the packet from his fingers and urging his briefs past his narrow hips. He had those sexy dents on either side of his butt, and her fingers trembled as she opened the wrapper. For a hot minute they were frozen, both ready for what was coming. And then it was happening.

On her back in the luxurious bed, she welcomed him inside of her. It had been a long time since she'd been with a man, and he was a big guy, but after a heart-stopping second her body adjusted and bliss soon began to spread through her.

"Ah, Joy." He held himself up on his strong arms, rotating his hips just right to send her higher. "Damn, baby. You feel...damn."

Joy couldn't speak beyond moans rising in volume as he picked up the tempo. She could do nothing but hold on for the ride, her hands tight on his biceps as she arched toward him. She came then, over and over as he kept up the pleasure. It was like flying around the room, out the balcony doors and up to those gorgeous stars.

As if from far away, she heard him groaning now. Delicious, evocative sounds that sent her soaring again.

"Oh, Zach." She stretched up and kissed his mouth, catching more of his heated moans. "Oh, my."

"Joy, baby."

He buried his face in the crook of her neck, the bristly stubble on his jaw adding to the sensations overwhelming her now. She crested again and he joined her, his big body shuddering as he held her closer still.

Their breath mingled and she held him tight, her hands stroking his smoothly muscled back. Her pulse began to slow and the sheen of sweat on their bodies seemed to cool.

"Jingles, that was amazing," he said, cupping her face and kissing her softly.

She caught her breath at the tenderness in his eyes. "You're amazing, Cowboy."

He smiled and gently withdrew. That lovely coverlet at the end of the bed covered them once more, and she pillowed her head on his chest.

"I wanted to wish for this," she admitted on a whisper. "Out there on the balcony."

"You did?" He turned his head to gaze down at her. "On a star, I'll bet."

She smiled a little. "What else?"

He tapped the tip of her nose, and then kissed her again. "There's bushels of mistletoe all over this place, Joy. Maybe you just wanted me to do more than kiss you."

Her smile widened and she shifted to rest her chin on her hands. "What, like that…snow job I gave you last night?"

He barked out a laugh. "Good one, Jingles." His eyes sparkled at her. "I don't think I'll ever hear those words again without thinking about these perfect lips and just how crazy they make me."

She still saw shadows in his eyes, and took a breath before forging ahead. "Do you want to talk about it, Zach? About what you felt when you saw your mother today?"

He closed his eyes for a minute, his thick lashes shadows on his cheekbones, and then faced her again. "I felt like I was a kid again, Joy. That kid who came home to find his mother gone."

"You're not that little boy anymore, Zach. You're a man who has made his own way in the world."

"Did I? I worked my father's ranch, baby. Maybe not like in the hired hand way we all treated Billy, but it wasn't my choice."

"I thought you and Chase lived and breathed that ranch.

He's always talking about the horses and cows."

"Cattle," he corrected with a smile as he always did, which was why she'd said it that way. "He and I made the ranch a moneymaker, sure. Even before Wild Harry passed, we'd taken over the business side of things. Our father was always better with animals than people."

It broke her heart, the way he talked about his father's remoteness. Added with his mother's desertion? It was a wonder that he didn't just hunker down in that ranch and live out a life of loneliness.

"You're different from them, you know." He started to shake his head but she touched his cheek to stop the movement. "You're not remote like your father, Zach. I've seen the connection between you and Chase, and when you talk about Billy there's a warmth there."

He brushed his hair back, and tucked his arm under his head. "Maybe."

She wouldn't push him. This was all so new, for him and for her. So she stretched out on top of him and kissed him until they were both lost in each other again.

Later, as he held her close, she wondered about a woman who could just walk away from her children. She ran her gaze over Zach's profile, seeing the beauty that had grabbed her and inspired her new artistic spark. He was funny and sweet, and not at all the distant guy he'd said he was.

That woman doesn't know what she missed.

***

"That's all there is to it, Mr. Harris." Darby looked over at Chase, who wore an open expression. "Mr. Harris, you both just need to sign every place I've put a little flag."

She sounded very excited and if Zach were being completely honest he was eager to get this whole thing over and done with. He thumbed through the copies and signed or initialed where it said to, passing the papers one at a time to his brother.

"They had no problem with any of our changes?" Chase asked Darby.

"Not at all," she said. "They're relieved that you won't be taking more furniture with you."

"My wife said she was looking forward to picking stuff out for our new place herself," Chase said with a chuckle. "I don't blame her. All of this stuff is pretty worn."

Zach nodded his agreement, sliding over another sheet of paper. "I won't miss a stick of it."

Chase and Darby both grew quiet but he just kept signing and initialing. When he was done, he set the pen down and sat back in his chair. Chase eyed him, and then added his signed papers to the stack beside Darby.

"When will the money hit?" he asked.

"On or about January second," she said. "I know it's a little bit later than we'd first thought, but with the holidays and everything? It's tough to schedule."

"But it's all set, right?" Zach asked.

Chase nudged him with his shoulder. "You'd think you were the one looking to settle down, bro."

Zach's belly clenched. Last night with Joy had been incredible, and not just the smoking hot sex. She was sweet, and just what he needed. He sure as hell wasn't ready to settle down, though.

"I just want this behind us," he said.

Darby slid all of the signed papers into her bag and stood. "We're all set then, gentlemen."

Chase and Zach stood, and she handed Chase a business card. "I'm working at the Sales Center in Cypress Corners now, so let me know when you and Carrie want to look at a few houses?"

Chase pocketed the card. "I sure will."

"Congratulations on the job," Zach said.

She smiled and Zach walked her to the front door.

"Are you still at the inn?" she asked him.

"I am," Zach said.

She tapped her chin and then nodded. "I might have seen a couple of places for you to look at, too."

"I'm not looking right now, but I'll let you know."

"Do that." She shouldered her bag. "There's something out there for everyone."

Zach didn't say anything to that. He shut the door behind her and went back into the kitchen.

"What was that about?" Chase asked.

"What?"

"You're not looking right now?" Chase scoffed. "You don't want to stay at the inn forever, do you?"

Zach bristled. "I've been there less than two weeks, Chase."

"But you're basically living with the Rollins family."

"I'm living at the inn, bro. Not with Joy's family."

His brother's brows rose. "You're dating, right?"

"We are."

"And she lives there, too?"

"Yep." Zach shoved his hands in his pockets. "What are you trying to say, Chase?"

Chase spun a kitchen chair around and straddled it. "Seems to me you have a pretty cozy situation there."

Zach put his hands on the table and leaned toward his brother. "Are you calling me a hound dog or saying Joy's easy?"

To his surprise, Chase laughed. "Neither, Zach. You need to chill."

Zach crossed to sink and filled a glass with water before taking a long drink. He'd put it off long enough. He had to tell Chase what happened yesterday morning.

"Bro, something's bugging you," Chase said. "Spill."

Zach turned to his brother again, leaning back against the sink. "I saw Mom yesterday."

The color drained from Chase's face. "What?" he rasped.

"She was in the town square." Zach let out a breath. "In front of the coffee shop."

"In Cypress Corners?" At Zach's nod, Chase let out a curse and slammed his fist down on the table. "What the fuck? Why is she out there?"

Zach shrugged. "I thought it might have something to do

with selling the ranch, but when this went through I knew that wasn't it."

Chase rubbed a hand over his face, his eyes looking wet. "I can't believe she came back here. She has to know we're living out in Cypress, Zach. Why the hell else would she be there?"

"I'm pretty sure Lettie Fairfax knew."

"Lettie?" Chase screwed up his face. "That sassy lady who sits in front of the coffee shop?"

"Yep. It seemed like she was trying to warn me yesterday. Before I ran into our mother."

"How the hell long has she been here, Zach?"

"I have no idea."

Chase studied the tabletop, running his fingertips over a few of the scratches. "It's been over twenty years, Zach."

His brother's voice was thick, and Zach crossed to him and placed a hand on his shoulder. "Yep."

There really wasn't anything more to say to Chase's statement. It had been a long damn time since she'd left, and he was still trying to deal with this blast from the past himself.

"Do you think she's going to try to make contact with me, too?"

"I would guess so, bro. I'm sorry to say, but we have to

find out just what she's doing here."

Chase stood, shaking his head. "I'm not going down that road. Nuh uh."

"I just wanted you to know before the Holiday Festival this weekend, man. I didn't want her to catch you off guard, too."

Chase wore a mix of emotions on his face, hurt and curiosity and anger. Zach flashed back to that afternoon they'd come home and found their mother gone. He'd been mad and hurt, but Chase had cried long and loud all night. As for their father? Wild Harry hadn't said a damn thing to make his sons feel better.

"Thanks, bro." Chase breathed in, straightening. "I'll know to look out for her."

They both, without more conversation, decided to put the subject aside and instead talked about the stables Zach was working on with Billy.

"Do you think horseback riding lessons would work out there?" Zach asked.

"I do! It's a damn good idea, bro."

Then they locked up the house for what was probably the last time. They each got in their trucks, and he waved a hand as Chase drove off down the drive. Zach sat there for a long time, staring up at his family's old home. It looked empty, but then it always had. He tried to think of a time when their mother had been happy there, but he just kept picturing her sitting quietly in the living room.

He'd liked it when she'd help him with his reading, though. It was one of the few warm memories he had of her in this house. He had several more of them, but they were of the times after she'd left.

He and his brother tossing a baseball back and forth out in the dusty afternoons. Learning to ride and rope from their father. Wishing every night when he went to bed that he'd wake up in the morning to find his mother in the kitchen making breakfast.

He wasn't that little kid anymore. He wouldn't wish for something that could never happen. Joy, that sweet and sexy woman of his, was more that he deserved. He was going to hold on to her, though. For as long as his luck held.

"Screw wishing."

He started the truck and headed back to Cypress Corners.

Chapter 16

Joy brushed her hair back from her face, eyeing a sleeping Zach beside her. It wasn't the first time she'd been with him in his room since Sunday night, but it was the first time She'd fallen asleep there. He'd tired her out for sure, and she'd all but passed out tucked into one of his super soft T-shirts. She was grateful that some internal clock woke her this morning.

It was Friday, the first day of the Holiday Festival, and she had lots to do. She had trouble looking away from him, though. He looked so relaxed there, one arm behind his head and the other resting on the white coverlet. The faint lines usually evident in his brow were smoothed and his sculpted lips were slightly parted. Tilting her head, she gazed at the profile that had started her down the new endeavor she was embarking on today.

He looked perfect to her. Heck, she figured he'd look perfect to just about any woman between the ages of eight and eighty. He was hers. For right now, at least.

Leaning over him, she brushed a kiss over his mouth and climbed out of bed. His hand encircled her wrist, keeping her standing there.

"Where are you going, Jingles?"

"It's already seven o'clock." She turned her wrist to grasp

his hand with hers. "I have to get ready for the festival, Cowboy."

He stretched and she couldn't resist staring at his chest and abs as the coverlet slipped down to his waist.

"I'm helping you, baby." His thumb stroked the back of her hand. "Between the framed art you made and your supplies, we'll need my truck."

"There are a lot of boxes downstairs, but despite the fact that Claire's dad fixed it I'm betting you still don't trust my Jeep. That's it, right?"

"No argument there. Do I need to remind you of Black Friday?"

"Nope." She grinned. "I almost enjoyed that ride back to Cypress Corners."

"Almost?" His eyes sparkled. "And what about last night's?"

Her body flushed as she recalled their most recent close encounter. "You better be careful, Zach. You're sure to land on the naughty list."

"That, Joy, is a small price to pay."

She brought his hand to her lips and dropped a kiss on his knuckles before releasing him. "Let me go get ready and I'll meet you downstairs?"

"Okay, then." He reached those lovely arms up over his head with a lusty groan. "I'll jump in the shower and see you in a few."

Before she could give in to the delicious notion of joining him in that spa-like shower, she pulled on her jeans and grabbed the rest of her clothes. "Okay if I get this back to you later?" she asked, holding out the bottom of the blue Florida Marlins shirt.

"No problem."

She kissed him again, because she could, and hurried out into the blessedly-empty hallway. By the time she was dressed in her casual elf outfit, consisting of another silly sweater and striped leggings, she was nervous and excited about the coming day. Since it was Friday, the festival wouldn't kick off until noon. Saturday and Sunday would be a different story, but today was her big debut.

In the grand scheme of things, she was a little fish in the Cypress fishbowl today. Caro Graham's bakery would do a brisk business, selling several new and favorite holiday treats. Joy would never tell her mother this to her face, but Caro's peppermint white chocolate almond biscotti was something she wouldn't miss. Other arts and crafts tents would be there, along with food trucks parked all along one side of the square. The tents were going up first, though. And she needed to be there so no one at the Sales Center would regret letting her slide in as a vendor at the last minute.

"Joy, I'm so happy you're doing this!" her mother said, surprising her with a hug from behind. "Your silhouettes are going to be a big hit."

Joy patted her hand and turned to face her. "I sure hope so."

"Is this something you might want to do long term? I mean, you could set up a storefront on the square."

"I don't know about that, but I do love the idea of working right here in Cypress."

Her mother positively beamed at that disclosure. "Your father would be very happy to hear that."

Joy choked up, placing a hand on her chest. "Thanks, Mom."

"What are you waiting for, Jingles?"

Both women looked over as Zach came down the staircase. He wore a thin sweater under his leather jacket, and looked very yummy. Her mother sighed softly before giving Joy another squeeze. "You'll need those broad shoulders today," she

213

whispered.

Joy stifled a laugh as Zach reached her. "Do you want to grab a cup of coffee first?"

He shook his head. "Let's wait for Cool Beans." He winked. "I'll even buy you a peppermint mocha."

"You're on."

They loaded everything into the bed of his truck and headed out. It was chilly but clear this morning, and excitement made her a little jumpy. Her knees bounced as he parked on the square. The streets would be closed by ten, but right now it looked like most of the vendors were unloading and setting up.

"Easy there, Jingles." He squeezed her left thigh. "It'll be great."

She bit her lip and turned to him. "I hope so." Sucking in a breath, she straightened her shoulders. "Let's do this."

He smiled, and she was glad to give him this to think about today. Ever since Sunday night, she'd caught a melancholy expression on his face now and then. There had been no more run-ins with his mother so far, but today was the festival. If the woman was in Cypress Corners, she was bound to attend today.

Her booth was across the street from the bakery and very near the Sales Center. It was a pretty good spot, in her opinion.

Dancing a little to the Christmas carols now coming over the sound system wired all around the square, she spread a tablecloth over the table.

"How about that coffee?" Zach asked as he opened up a few folding chairs.

"Sounds great."

He grasped the back of her neck and kissed her. "Be right back."

She studied his face, seeing the apprehension in his gaze. That was where he'd seen his mother, of course. He was a big, strong guy. The smile she sent him was meant as one of encouragement and he gave a short nod.

As he walked across the street she set up her little work station. A chair for the subject to sit. Check. A chair for her to sit, set beside the table. Check. Cashbox and tablet for payments. Check. She unloaded some of her designs and then began to prop up some of the framed silhouettes on the table. She'd created an A-frame sign, and set that out on the sidewalk.

Glancing over at the samples she'd created, her gaze fell on Zach's silhouette. There was no stopping what would happen. She knew that. He would see his mother or he wouldn't. She knew something else, too.

No matter what he needed from her? She would give it wholeheartedly.

***

Zach crossed his arms and watched as Joy worked. The kids seemed to love her, and their parents were all clamoring to get silhouettes done of their children. It had been like this since right before noon, and she was in her element.

A few of the Cypress people nodded to him, and he vaguely recognized more of them than he might have expected. Joy, however, was familiar with just about everybody who walked by.

It was almost two o'clock and he'd lost count of the number of people she'd cut, or whatever the exact word was. He framed the pieces and took the cash or entered the credit card info into her tablet.

"Can we get on the list, bro?"

Zach looked over at his brother and Carrie, and then down at the little beauty in the stroller. "Isn't Caitlyn a little young for this?"

"Oh, I hope not." Carrie walked over to where Joy sat and watched for a little bit as she cut a likeness of a dark-haired boy who looked to be about seven years old sitting in front of her.

"Joy, can you do babies?"

"If you hold her, sure." Joy bit her lip, tilting her head in that way he found very cute as she put the finishing touches on the silhouette. "I can do one with both of you."

Carrie clasped her hands. "Oh, yay! Chase, write us down."

Chase wrote on the list, whistling loudly. "Looks like you've been busy."

"She's good," Zach said.

Joy looked over at him, beaming as she finished. She turned in the chair and glued the cut-out to the thick paper and held it up toward the little boy. "What do you think, Nick?"

The boy grinned, fisting his hands to keep from touching it as he checked it out. "It's really cool. Dad, check this out!"

The kid's father, a tall broad guy with black hair, looked down at the silhouette. "That's very cool, Nick."

Joy smiled. "Thanks, Rick." She stood and waved Zach over. "Rick, I want you to meet Zach Harris. Zach, this is Rick Chapman."

Zach shook the guys hand. "Nice to meet you."

"Rick runs the Sales Center." Joy crossed her arms and nodded. "He's the reason I was able to get a booth on such late notice."

Rick shook his head. "You're proposal was a good one, Joy. There hasn't been anything like this at one of our events." He smiled. "It was no trouble making room for you."

"And I just love this!" A pretty blond with long, curly hair walked up to stand beside the boy. "Nick, this is great."

"She did it with scissors, Mom." Nick's eyes were large. "Can I watch her do another one?"

"It's okay with me, Harmony," Joy said. "Zach, this is Harmony. Rick's wife."

Zach nodded to her. "Nice to meet you."

Harmony narrowed her eyes a little bit. "Boy, there's no mistaking that you and Chase are brothers."

Chase laughed as he walked over to slap Zach on the back. "No mistaking a Harris. That's for sure."

"Zach, I wanted to talk to you about the stables you and Billy are planning out on the east side of the property," Rick said. "One of our new salespeople mentioned it. Darby said your ranch out in St. Cloud was just beautiful."

Zach nodded. "What do you think of the project?"

"I think it'll be a slam dunk. Visitors have been asking about exploring the wilder parts of Cypress on horseback."

"There are trails for biking and walking already," Harmony put in. "The Institute would love to partner with you and Billy on widening the trails to allow four-legged residents."

Zach smiled. "I'll get with Billy and we'll set a time to come by."

"Just call or text me." Rick handed Zach a card. "Mr. Forbes, the developer, will want to sit in. And my brother Ben will definitely want a hand in the design."

"I'll bow to your recommendations, for sure," he said. "I want this to fit into Cypress."

"And you, too?" his sister-in-law asked.

"Yep." He winked at Joy, seeing the happy surprise on her face.

Carrie beamed a smile at Chase and lifted the baby, who was dressed in a little one-piece sweater thing with reindeer running across it. She settled in the chair in front of Joy, holding the baby in front of her. Zach had been very impressed when Joy had done her first two-person silhouette. He'd seen her do dozens by now, but it was still pretty cool to watch. He could definitely identify with Nick Chapman.

"Are you ready, Carrie?"

Chase's wife nodded. Joy directed her where to look and

then waited patiently as the baby squirmed a little on her mother's lap. Carrie cooed in one of Caitlyn's tiny ears as she managed to keep her relatively still for Joy.

"That is pretty cool," Chase said to Zach in a low voice. "But I bet you're watching the artist more than the art?"

Zach chuckled, turning to face his brother. Then he froze. There across the street, just in front of the bakery, stood their mother.

"Chase," he said, his voice low.

"What?" Chase was still grinning as he straightened. "You know I'm only kidding around, bro."

Zach gave a small shake of his head. "Over there."

Chase's brows drew together, and then he froze. "Damn. It's her."

Carrie grew quiet and Joy stiffened. Both women watched them, but Zach squared his shoulders. "Maybe she won't... Shit, she's coming over."

He had the chance to watch his mother crossing toward them. She was dressed in a pair of dark pants and a sweater, looking like any of the other older women he'd seen around town. She wore a frown on her face though, and her eyes searched them out. Her gaze zeroed in first on Chase and then on him. From the corner of his eye he watched Joy finish up the baby's silhouette and Carrie hefted the baby up on her shoulder and joined them.

"That's her, isn't it?" she asked Chase.

Zach wasn't surprised that his brother had shared this with his wife. Hell, he'd told Joy hadn't he? Joy told a couple of people waiting to sign in that it would be a little while and came to stand next to him. The touch of her hand on his arm went a long way toward relaxing his muscles, which he hadn't been aware had tightened.

"Hello," his mother said, a small smile on her face. "It's so good to see you both."

Chase mumbled something under his breath that Zach didn't quite catch but Zach just stared her down.

"Hello," he bit out.

She flinched almost imperceptibly, and turned toward Carrie. "That baby is just adorable!"

"Thank you." Carrie's voice was soft but held none of the warmth he'd come to expect. "Chase, I'll see you over at the bakery."

She hustled the baby away, one hand pushing the empty stroller as she made her exit. Joy didn't move, though. Their mother turned to face her now.

"Helen Snow."

So she'd gone back to her maiden name. Zach wasn't really surprised.

His mother smiled. "Joy Rollins, isn't it?"

"Yes."

Helen licked her lips and made a show of looking at Joy's work. "These are really remarkable, Joy. Lettie Fairfax told me you were quite the artist."

"Lettie's a good friend," Joy said, her tone clipped.

"What do you want?" Zach asked.

Helen blinked as she faced him. "I…" She looked over at Chase, a smile pulling at her mouth. "I just wanted to say hello."

"You said it." Chase stalked off across the street where Carrie and the baby were waiting.

His mother looked back at Zach. "I thought we could talk."

Zach grunted. "I have nothing to say to you."

"You're not going to leave like your brother did?" Helen asked.

"This is Joy's thing," he said. "I'm here for her. You'll have to be the one to leave. It's what you're good at, right?"

His mother winced, but she pasted on a false smile. "Joy, it was nice meeting you."

Joy dipped her head but didn't say anything more.

Helen left, and it was all Zach could do to stay on his feet. His face felt hot and his hands and feet cold. Was this what you felt like before passing out? He'd only been knocked out once in his life, in high school when a hitter batted a line drive right to his belly. This felt a lot like that. He was having trouble breathing, and only Joy's hand on him was keeping him upright.

"It's okay," she whispered. "You saw her again and you lived through it."

He looked over at her, at those big brown eyes of hers, and his lungs expanded. "Thanks, baby."

She didn't say anything more, but she reached up to stroke her fingers through his hair. It was a small gesture, but one he'd noticed she liked to do when he kissed her. He wanted to kiss her right now, but it wasn't the time or the place.

Later, when he got her alone again, he'd show her just how grateful he was for this support. Shaking it off, he announced that people could sign in for silhouettes and business picked up again.

Joy caught his eye throughout the afternoon, and every time he felt that shift in his chest. When had he come to rely on her so much? Again he was seized with the worry that he'd do something to send her running from him. Like his mother had.

He wouldn't focus on that. No. He had his Jingles and he was going to keep her. For as long as he could.

Chapter 17

Saturday night, Joy was pleasantly exhausted. The festival had been crowded and her booth very busy, but between Zach's company and a steady supply of peppermint biscotti, the day passed quickly. More importantly, there had been no sign of his mother.

"Pizza tonight, Jingles?" Zach wrapped his arms around her, kissing her ear. "In my room?" he added on a whisper.

Tingles coursed through her. They'd been together just about every night since that first time yet just one touch, one word, and she was so ready for more. Not just sexually, though that was beyond anything she could have imagined. They seemed to be connecting more and more.

"Sounds like a date, Cowboy." She wrapped her hands around his wrists. "I'll even let you pick the toppings."

He kissed her neck and stepped back. "You must be hungry. Meat, meat and meat?"

"That would be just about perfect."

Carrie Harris walked up then. "Hey, Zach."

"Hey there, Carrie," he answered.

"Joy, can I talk to you two a second?" Carrie asked.

Joy and Zach exchanged a look but she knew that he could

read the concern on Carrie's face.

"What's going on?" Zach asked.

Carrie took in a breath, obviously steeling herself for something. "I invited Helen to dinner tomorrow night. At the tavern."

Joy was stunned but Zach looked poleaxed.

"What the hell, Carrie?" he asked. "Does Chase know?"

"It was his idea. Kind of." She shrugged. "After I told him it would do him good."

Zach shook his head, thunderclouds in his eyes. "Yep. You tell yourself that, Carrie."

"Zach, won't you come?" Carrie asked. "Joy, you're invited too."

Joy held up her hands. "This is a family thing, Carrie. You and Chase and Zach."

Carrie blinked at her. "Aren't you two…? You're an item, as Lettie would say."

"Joy's mine and I'm hers."

Joy looked at Zach and then back at Carrie. "I'm not going to drag Zach to dinner, Carrie."

Carrie frowned. "I don't blame you. I'd hoped that this could be a good start."

"You'll just have to find out without me," Zach said. As Carrie started to go, Zach touched her shoulder. "Don't count on her to hang around, Carrie. It's not in her."

"You don't know that, Zach," Carrie said. "Not for sure."

Zach didn't say anything more. Joy waved to Carrie and then went back to packing up the booth for tomorrow.

"If you change your mind I'll go with you," she said at last.

Zach crossed his arms, the look on his face impassive. "I'm not going to play that, Joy. Maybe it's her guilty conscience. Maybe it's the holidays. I don't care either way. I'm not going to have anything to do with that woman."

Joy hugged him now, resting her cheek against his chest. He might seem unmoved but she heard his heart pounding beneath her ear.

"I'm with you, Zach."

His arms came around her and they stood there for a long minute. "You promise?"

It was softly asked, that startling question. The words, his voice, tugged at her in ways she hadn't expected.

She looked up to find him staring at her, and smiled. "I promise."

His arms tightened around her. "Thanks."

He stepped back from her and cleared his throat. "Now let's get this done, Jingles. I'm starving, and for more than pizza from the tavern."

Joy took her cue from him and kept things light as they returned to the inn.

Sunday dawned bright and clear, perfect for the last day of the festival. After last night's dinner, and last night spent in Zach's bed, Joy was pleased that none of that melancholy seemed to cling to him this morning.

"How about that shower, baby?" he asked, stretching as he got out of bed.

"Sounds good."

She sat up and watched as he went into the bathroom. It never ceased to amaze her that he was completely comfortable walking around naked. She sure didn't mind gazing at this living Greek statue. She was a bit less self-conscious herself now, too. The hungry looks he gave her more than made up for any misgivings on her part. Joining him in the shower, they were soon squeaky clean and very satisfied.

"Another day another dollar, Jingles." He toweled his hair as she got dressed. "Have you thought about what you're going to do after the holidays? With your art, I mean?"

Joy paused. "I'm not sure. I can see doing the silhouettes at the inn on the weekends, but it's not exactly anything to build a fortune on."

He nodded and pulled a shirt over his head. How was it that watching him dress was almost as sexy as watching him undress?

"I thought you could work with me," he said.

"Doing what exactly?" She walked up to him, snaking an arm around his neck. "Are you looking for a concubine?"

He chuckled. "Nope. I'm pretty happy with my current situation. Maybe you could help me with lessons out at the stables."

Alarm trilled through her and she stepped back. "I'm not so good with horses, Zach."

"So you've said. I was thinking more about the kids, Joy. I'm about as good with them as you are with horses."

"You're wrong. I saw you with all of the kids who came to the booth over the past two days, Zach. You're very good with them. You talk to them like they're people."

He smiled. "Aren't they?"

"Yes, but a lot of adults talk down to them."

"I liked most of the little cowpokes."

An idea struck her. "That's what you should call them!"

"Who?"

"Your students at the stables. Cypress Corners Cowpokes."

"Billy would probably like that." He chuckled. "I'll think about it."

"Let me go finish getting dressed and we'll meet downstairs?"

He kissed her and nodded. "Run, Jingles. And after today? We're going to talk about the future."

She left him to grab some fresh clothes from her room, not even thinking about what he'd said. She didn't know what to do with that particular promise.

***

Zach stood outside the Sales Center on Monday morning, looking over the town square. Things looked pretty normal after the chaos that had been the Holiday Festival, at least normal for Cypress Corners. It was still dressed like a crazy Christmas card, but that didn't seem to bug him any longer.

"Must be Jingles," he murmured.

She sure as hell had made a place in his life. Fit damn good there, too. Yesterday he'd even said the F-word. *The Future*, with a capital F. He'd meant the lessons out at the stables, but after seeing both the warmth and heat she gave him before she'd left his room? That had him thinking about other things, too.

"Hey there, Zach Harris."

Zach turned to see Jessie Brady bounding up the steps. "Hey, Jessie."

"Rick said you'd be in today to talk about the stables. I'm not afraid to say that the salespeople are chomping at the bit to talk about that in their tours." She laughed at her own joke.

Zach smiled. "I'm looking forward to hearing your boss's ideas for the project."

"Prepare yourself," she said. "Once Rick gets behind a project, it's full steam ahead." She screwed up her face. "Hmm. I can't think of a horse metaphor for that one."

"Like a stampede of wild horses?" Jessie laughed again and Zach pulled open the door for her. "A little on the nose, right?"

Her eyes widened. "Zach, you're different. Now."

"Am I?"

She nodded. "Oh, yes. And I think a certain Christmas elf has something to do with that."

"You might be right on that count, Pixie," he said, using just about everybody's nickname for her.

She grinned and rushed past him through the reception area and down a hall to the left. An older woman about his mother's age smiled at him from behind the reception desk.

"Good morning, Mr. Harris," she said. "Rick Chapman and Mr. Forbes are expecting you."

"Thank you…"

"Sharon Walsh. I'm Ty's mother. You've met my son, haven't you?"

"I don't think so, ma'am. Not yet, anyway."

"You will. He's the Wildlife Tech out here." She wore an expression of pride on her face. "He'll probably be taking you on an eco-tour soon."

"You bet he will." Rick Chapman stepped into the lobby. "Good morning, Zach."

"Hi, Rick." Zach nodded to Ty's mother. "Very nice meeting you, Mrs. Walsh."

"You too, son."

He stifled a shiver at her words, feeling like a goose walked over him or something like that. Joy would know the exact phrase. His girl knew just about everything.

"Come on down to the conference room, Zach." Rick began to walk down the hallway and Zach followed. "My brother Ben wanted to sit in."

"The architect, right?"

Rick chuckled. "Yes. Seems he can't wait to put in his two cents on the project."

"He did a fine job on Billy and Shannon's farmhouse," Zach said. "Billy should be here in a few minutes."

"I imagine the mornings are busy for him out at the farm." Rick waved him into the conference room. "It must seem strange, not working at your ranch any longer."

"I'm getting used to it."

"Hello, Mr. Harris." A fifty-something man with a neat moustache, salt-and-pepper and a serious expression stuck out his hand. "I'm Mr. Forbes."

Zach shook his hand. "Nice to meet you, Mr. Forbes. You've done some amazing things with this development."

He flashed a smile before sobering. "No man is an island, Mr. Harris. I have a crack team around me."

Zach nodded. "I'm eager to hear what they think of our little project."

"All good, my boy." Mr. Forbes sat and Rick and Zach did likewise. "All good."

"Good morning." A guy who looked a lot like Rick walked

into the conference room. "Ben Chapman."

Zach shook his hand. "Nice to meet you."

"You, too." Ben sat down. "What have you got so far, bro?"

Rick arched a brow and looked at Zach. "I guess this isn't going to be a very formal meeting."

Ben laughed. "Not today, Rick. We're talking about stables and horses. Time to loosen your tie, right Zach?"

Zach shrugged. He'd worn a shirt and tie this morning, and it was feeling a little less like a tight lasso at the moment. The Chapmans were as friendly as Joy had told him, and he was feeling more comfortable by the minute. When Billy joined them, wearing a grin and also a shirt and tie, Zach was happy he'd decided to partner with his cousin.

They both shared their plans and expectations for the venture, playing off of each other's comments almost as easily as if they'd practiced it. Billy had a sound business mind, and he was gifted with animals. Zach couldn't think of a better guy to work on this, and it was a good thing that he wouldn't have any more responsibilities at Harris Ranch. He planned to give all of his attention to the project, since Billy had the goat farm to run too.

"How big will this project be?" Mr. Forbes asked them.

Zach looked to Billy, who brought up their preliminary specs on his tablet. Ben and Mr. Forbes both nodded, and then Rick began to ask about the particulars regarding lessons, staffing, etc.

"I'll be teaching," Zach said. "I hope to bring on a couple more people at least when we open."

"You'll need more than a couple if this is as successful as I anticipate," Rick said.

"I'm thinking of having Joy Rollins work with the kids," Zach said.

Ben's brows rose, and then he nodded. "She would be terrific with the children."

"I think so, too. Nick's had her as a substitute a few times, and really liked her." Rick folded his hands on the table. "Have you thought about student volunteers?"

Zach looked at Billy, who didn't seem to know the answer either.

"You mean, the kids?" Zach asked.

"High schoolers," Rick said. "We're out here in rural Osceola County, Zach. I'm sure you know that lots of the kids at Cypress Corners High have horses and farming in their blood."

"I guess that's true," Zach said.

"Over at the high school they have the Four-H of course, but I was thinking about the exceptional students. The Cypress Institute employs a couple kids, and they often come on the eco-tours with Ty."

"High schoolers?" Zach thought for a minute. He'd taken some reading classes with a few kids from the special-education department, and he'd found they were both friendly and hardworking. "That might be a great idea, actually."

"I'll give you the name of Ty's contact over at the school," Rick said.

"Thanks, Rick." He and Billy exchanged a look and his cousin looked like he was pretty satisfied with what was discussed this morning.

"Now on to the design," Ben Chapman said. "How large do you think you'll need?"

"I was thinking about ten stalls, with a good-sized tack room at the back," Zach said.

"We're going to get some of the miniature horses for the petting zoo, and I thought Zach could use those for the littler kids," Billy said.

A smile broke across Ben's face. "I bet Tammy would love

a picture of Raffaella on one of those."

Zach filed that idea away as another way to entice Joy to come and work at the stables. She had that artist's eye of hers, and would probably love photographing the little ones on equally little horses.

Some more details were nailed down as Ben took note of Zach and Billy's specs. Before long the meeting concluded, and the men parted with plans to get together again once Ben finished his preliminary design. Zach accompanied Billy outside.

"I have to tell you, cuz," Billy began. "I'm getting excited about this."

"You and me both," Zach said.

Billy shook his hand. "Come out to the farmhouse tonight, Zach. We'll have dinner and can go over everything."

Zach nodded, and then he spotted Joy across the street. She was wearing another one of those crazy holiday sweaters of hers, and her hair was up on a ponytail. She rocked that cute/sexy thing and bounced on the balls of her feet.

As he waved to her, Billy nudged his shoulder. "Bring Joy."

Zach started and faced his cousin. "Yeah?" At Billy's nod, he smiled. "Okay. Will do."

She smiled and waved back at Zach, and he felt his heart thump. That was something that happened more and more often lately, but he wouldn't wonder why at the moment. It felt too damn good right now.

Chapter 18

"Dinner was great, Shannon." Joy helped her hostess carry some of the dishes into the kitchen. "Thanks so much for inviting me."

Shannon started rinsing a few dishes, and then stopped for a beat. "You know, I never really cooked much before I got married. Billy cooks sometimes, but usually only if it involves fire."

Billy walked over to the fridge to grab three bottles of beer. "Hey, I grill, Shannon. When we need meat, I make fire."

"Which is every day," Zach put in as he joined them. "Not that your pasta wasn't delicious, Shannon."

"Thanks for that, Zach." She smirked at Billy. "See? Not everyone needs meat at every meal."

"I'm afraid that's a product of having grown up on a ranch." Zach took a bottle from Billy and draped his arm over Joy's shoulders. "Wild Harry insisted on meat at every meal."

"That's no joke," Chase said as he came into the kitchen. "Baby's almost down, Shannon. Carrie said she needs coffee."

"You got it." Shannon turned on the coffee maker and went back to loading the dishwasher.

"It's not too late for coffee?" Joy asked.

Chase shrugged. "Caitlyn still gets up in the middle of the night. Carrie's afraid she'll sleep through it." He barked out a short laugh. "Not that I've ever been able to."

"So did Billy tell you about our stables, Chase?" Zach asked.

"I heard something about it." Chase opened his beer and sat on one of the barstools at the tall counter. "Should be a pretty good business."

"Joy's going to work with the little ones," Billy said.

Joy straightened in surprise. "I am?"

Zach gave her a squeeze. "Just something we talked about in the meeting today, Jingles. Billy's getting some miniature horses and Ben Chapman had an idea for pictures with the kids. Sitting on them. Maybe riding them around the paddock."

Joy nibbled on her lower lip. "I guess ponies are less scary than horses."

"Miniature horses," Zach said. "Not ponies."

"Potato, potahto," Shannon said with a laugh.

Billy reached over and tweaked Shannon's nose. "That's what we get for getting involved with city girls."

"What's this about city girls?" Carrie asked as she joined them.

"Just talking about what greenhorns you three ladies are," Chase said with a grin.

Shannon and Carrie laughed and Joy felt a warmth spread through her. She was part of this group? She was a greenhorn involved with a Harris? Not too shabby.

When Zach's hand dropped to rest on her hip, she leaned into him. This was amazing, this connection between them. It was almost a physical thing. And her circle of friends was growing to include all these Harris folks. She'd been right when she'd told Zach it wasn't really a circle, though. It wasn't closed off at all.

A little while later, Zach drove her back to the inn.

"You don't mind that I said you'd be working with me?" he asked her. "I mean, we only talked a little bit about it this morning."

"I'm surprised, but in a good way." She reached over and squeezed his bicep. "This is something I hadn't thought of, the ponies." She winked at him. "But I think it could be fun."

"Fun?" Zach's lips curved at one corner. "Jingles, I can't believe you need to be reminded just what fun is."

"Zach Harris, I thought you were Scrooge when I met you."

"You did?"

She snorted. "Please. You said just about everything but bah humbug about Christmas."

His eyes sparkled as he glanced over at her for a second. "I was told today by a Pixie that a certain elf changed me."

Joy's heart clenched and she covered it with one hand. "Me?" Her throat grew tight, but she smiled anyway. "That's amazing."

"What's amazing?" He squeezed her thigh. "That I changed? Or that you changed me?"

"Both?"

"You asking or telling there, Jingles?"

She faced him even though he was still focused on driving. "Telling, Cowboy. Now how about showing me some of that fun you were talking about?"

He growled softly in the back of his throat. "I'll show you, baby."

Her body was humming in anticipation by the time they made it to Zach's room. They didn't quite make it to the bed, but instead got down to some naked fun right in front of the crackling fireplace.

"I could get used to this, Jingles." He kissed her throat, her breasts. "Taking you back to my place."

His words, his magical touch, made her weak with wanting.

"Zach." She sucked in a breath as pleasure began to rise. "You can take me anywhere."

He brought his face to hers, his eyes sparkling. "Do you mean that?"

Her mind tried to grasp what he was saying, but his hands and the rest of his big body were driving her slightly crazy.

"Zach, please."

"Sure thing, baby." He kissed her, hard, and then moved to give her everything.

After, once they'd come down from that amazing ride, Joy thought about everything he'd said. And what he hadn't. They'd made their way onto the bed at some point, and he'd loved her every which way. Her hands and knees had tangled in the sheets as he drove into her from behind. His hands had held tightly to her waist as she'd ridden him just as hard as he'd done her.

"Zach," she began, stretching out beside him in that languid afterglow. "What did you mean, exactly? About your place?"

He turned his head towards her, a searching look in his

eyes. "I have this stables thing going with Billy now, and there's the money from the sale of the ranch, but I felt like I was in limbo before I picked you up on the side of the road."

She moved onto her side, propping her head on one hand. "What are you saying, Cowboy?"

"I don't know much right now, Jingles. But I know I want to spend time with you. Only you. Do you have that going on?"

"Is this about my working out at the stables?"

"A little, but it's more about what we've been dancing around."

Her heart tripped and she couldn't help but smile. "Are you saying you're my boyfriend now?" It felt a little silly, but it was a declaration she'd never expected from him. "Is that it?"

He licked his lips and let out a breath. "Yep, it is. You're my girl, Joy. My girlfriend, I mean." He laughed lightly. "That's something I've never had before, let alone said."

"You've never had a girlfriend?" She snorted. "Yeah, right."

"It's true."

Her eyes pricked but she blinked back any tears. "Then I'm honored."

His smile was wide and bright and he hugged her to him.

"You're something else, Jingles." He kissed the top of her head. "And you're all mine.

***

Zach left the Cypress Institute with Ty Walsh early Friday morning, after deflecting some teasing from Joy's sister Becky at the reception desk. He'd shared a word or two with the director of the Institute, Dr. Robbins, too. The guy had a real absent-minded professor thing going on, but it was clear to Zach that the man knew his stuff and was all about his commitment to Cypress Corners. This eco-tour with Ty, though, was something Zach had been looking forward to, not that his second meeting with Ben Chapman yesterday hadn't been great in its own way.

The drawings he'd made of the stables put on paper exactly what Zach had envisioned. Billy had left this aspect of the project in Zach's hands, and Zach was pretty pleased with how it had been progressing.

His relationship with Joy was doing a lot of that, too. Progressing. She was his girlfriend, which still felt weird to say out loud. He was a grown man, after all. Loving Joy though, holding her in his arms and even just talking to her, made him feel a sense of connection he'd surely missed out on for years. It felt like the time was right, though. This woman was the right one for him. And he was damned if he didn't think he was the right one for her, too. It might be wishful thinking on his part, but he was going to try his best to be that guy.

"Let's head out," Ty said, directing him toward the lot behind the Institute.

Ty was a big guy with a wide smile, and he was apparently as friendly as his mother had been behind the front desk of the Sales Center. He'd been raised in Central Florida, like Zach had been, but he seemed to have a love of nature and the wilder side of things where Zach was a rancher through and through.

"We're going to take the Gator," Ty said, leading the way toward where three of the sturdy vehicles were parked.

"I'm thinking we're going off-road?"

"Yep." Ty buckled in and waited for Zach to do the same. "This is still the best way to see the east side of the property."

"I'm guessing that's true, unless you head out on a horse."

Ty nodded and led the Gator off of the road and up onto the sandy trail leading away from the town square. "I think lots of folks might like to explore that way, Zach. You know, we can partner and offer eco-tours that way too."

"You ride?" Zach asked.

"Yep. I haven't been able to ride as much as I'd like since

taking this job, though."

"They keep you pretty busy?"

"Sure do." He smiled. "I wouldn't want it any other way. It's my dream job."

"How long have you worked at Cypress?"

"Going on three years now."

Zach nodded. He'd heard that Ty was married to a Chapman, the only daughter in the family. They both worked out here, Ty's wife helping her brother Jake out at the Adventure Trails Zach liked to use. It was apparently a family affair but every Chapman, from Rick to the little strawberry blond baby he now knew belonged to Jake and Claire, was as friendly as the next. It was little wonder that Joy loved living here. Even he was starting to feel that connection, no matter that he'd only been out here since Thanksgiving.

As they made their way toward the east, he just sat back and marveled. He'd known that the property was extensive, but Zach hadn't known just how far east Cypress Corners stretched.

"I didn't realize how wild it is out here," he said.

Ty nodded. "Seventy percent of the land is set aside for conservation. Even the golf course is a nature conserve."

"That's impressive."

Ty looked over at him and smiled. "It has a way, you know. Of grabbing a hold of you and not letting go."

"I believe you're right there," Zach said. "I'm actually thinking about settling down out here."

"I'd heard you're dating Joy Rollins." Ty held up one hand. "I'm not gossiping, just making a statement."

"Yep, we're dating." Zach gripped the rail at his side as the Gator dipped into a deep rut before righting itself. "She's pretty much the reason I want to stay out here. Her and my family."

"I think what you have planned for the stables is a sound idea, Zach. You and Billy will make a good go of it."

"Thanks, Ty."

Ty switched into tour guide mode then, pointing out the habitats of certain native animals and teaching a country boy like Zach a thing or two before they headed back to the town center.

"So do you think you can make some of these trails part of your lessons?" Ty asked as they pulled in back of the Cypress Institute.

"I think we just might. I can't think of a better way to explore out there than on horseback." Zach smiled. "No offense to this fine machine of yours."

Ty laughed and stepped out of the Gator. "No offense

taken." He held out a hand to Zach. "Great getting to know you a little bit better, man."

Zach shook his hand. "Thanks for the tour, Ty."

Ty pocketed the keys to the Gator and headed back into the Institute. It was nearly noon now, and Zach knew Joy that would need him back at the inn in a little bit. The Cookies with Santa event at the community school was this afternoon, the unofficial second holiday festival he'd heard so much about, and he'd let her talk him into playing St. Nick again. Hell, he could admit to himself that his Jingles could talk him into just about anything.

A couple of hours later he was suited up, beard and all, and sitting on a green velvet throne. It wasn't quite as homey as his usual place in the inn's parlor, but then again they were in the cafeteria of the school. The chatter was high-pitched and a little wild, but that could be due to the endless supply of sugar and chocolate chip cookies that the bakery had provided for the event.

His Jingles was there, of course. Right in the thick of things. The kids seemed to flock to her, and she lit up as she talked to each and every little one. There were crafts for them, and Joy was helping them make ornaments and Christmas cards. She used those tiny scissors of hers and cut the prettiest paper snowflakes he'd ever seen. It wasn't the silhouettes, but that wasn't a surprise. They weren't there five minutes before they realized that there would be no getting these kids to sit still today.

"Looks like Santa could use a cookie," Harmony Chapman said.

Zach smiled and just stopped himself from answering her. Catching himself, he simply nodded his white-haired head and made the bells on his hat ring. She set a plate of cookies with icing and sugar sprinkles, and he caught the scent of peppermint.

"Compliments of Sweet Escape," Harmony said.

He took a bite of a red-and-white cooking, his eyes nearly rolling as the sweet and hot taste hit his tongue. "Wow," he mumbled. "No wonder the bakery is always crowded."

Harmony laughed and then went back to where her son Nick was helping Joy with the arts and crafts. Zach munched the delicious cookie during his rare and highly anticipated breather between taking pictures with the kids. Joy's brother Tom was using the break in the action to flirt and tease a young woman across the way who was handing out more cookies to the parents and children.

It was a very crowded event, and he was surprised to see

several people wave hello to him. He just waved back, a big and grand gesture keeping in character, but he was amazed to realize how many people he knew here. Noah Brady and his lookalike son Max. Harmony and Rick's kid Nick. The other Chapmans and their little ones, not to mention Chase and Carrie with Caitlyn. It all looked so perfect, but he knew it wasn't perfect. It was real. For a second Zach wished he'd had the kind of holiday these kids would have this year.

By dinner time the event was over, not that the kids would eat much after the cookies and cocoa they'd had today. Once he was safely in the kindergarten classroom where he'd dressed earlier, he shed his Santa outfit. Joy joined him, sliding in and helping him pack up the costume.

"That was so much fun!" She was humming and the bells on her skirt were jangling. "Those kids wore me out."

"You looked like you were having a great time, Jingles."

"A great time? It was a blast." She stopped and beamed a smile. "I guess I do love working with them."

"That's what you should do, then."

"What I should do?"

"Teach, Joy." He brushed a loose lock of hair from her cheek and tucked it behind her ear. "Teach art to the kids."

She bit her lip in that way he liked and shrugged. "I don't know. I'd have to get a certificate or something. Wouldn't I?"

"I'm thinking you could work that out, baby." He stroked her cheek. "How about a pizza at the tavern tonight?"

She nodded and kissed him.

Chapter 19

Joy was still thinking about Zach's suggestion the next morning. Maybe she could teach art at the school. It might involve more schooling. Maybe that would get her to finally finish her graduate degree. Christmas was still over a week away, though. She'd think about it after the New Year.

"It's not anything I have to decide now," she said as she finished dressing in her room.

She'd slept tucked in Zach's big strong arms last night, and rose ready to start a busy weekend at the inn. There would be another photo op this afternoon, with her favorite St. Nick front and center. Then she would cut the silhouettes for those people who had made appointments through the website she'd linked to the *Cypress Corners Scoop's* page.

"Good morning," she said to her mother as she stepped into the dining room.

"Hello, dear." Her mother placed her hands on her hips and surveyed the crowded room. "What do you think about this, Joy? Do you think your father would be happy?"

"He'd be thrilled." Joy poured herself a cup of coffee. "Are you ready for today?"

"Today is all about the photo op, dear." Her mother gave a

sharp nod. "No festival to compete with this weekend."

"That's true. Didn't you have a nice time at the festival?"

"Yes, yes." She waved a hand. "Sharon Walsh and I sat with Lettie for a while. Seems there's no keeping you and Zach a secret."

Joy searched her mother's face for any sign of disapproval. She might be a grown woman, but she still didn't want to thumb her nose at her mom.

"Are you okay with that?" Joy asked. "You know, with our relationship?"

Her mother's eyes twinkled and the Mrs. Claus façade was complete, in Joy's opinion. "Sweetheart, I've never seen you like this. You're so darn happy! And he's a good man."

"I think so."

"Then it's serious?"

Joy's heart thumped. "Serious? I don't know about that. I know we're exclusive."

"Then that will have to do. For now."

"For now?"

"You'll figure these things out, dear." Her mother squeezed Joy's upper arms and then gave then a firm pat. "He will, too."

Zach joined them then, and Joy did her best not to blush as he talked to her mother about the upcoming photo op. She busied herself with grabbing the two remaining cinnamon rolls for her and Zach and escaped into the parlor away from the crowd. Zach joined her with two mugs of coffee soon after.

"Great idea, Jingles." He set the mugs on the table beside her laptop. "I'm thinking this will be the last chance for us to be alone for a while today."

They ate their breakfast and shared kisses that tasted as delicious as her mother's trademark pastries before the whirlwind began.

By the time the weekend was over, she was pleasantly exhausted. The photo ops on Saturday and Sunday had been very busy, and she'd cut so many silhouettes than she could hardly count them all.

"Just a few more days, Jingles." Zach took her hand as they walked through the holiday crowds at the mall up in Orlando on Monday night. "Thanks so much for coming Christmas shopping with me."

She looked down at the bags he held, emblazoned with the logo of one of the biggest sports stores in the mall. "Seems like you had no problem shopping for Chase and Billy."

"Nah, they're easy. It's Shannon and Carrie where I'm clueless. Not to mention little carrottop."

"That's what I'm here for, Cowboy." She held tightly to his hand and wrapped her other hand around his arm. "Never fear."

He gave a dramatic shiver. "Just don't drag me into that hot pink underwear store."

She laughed and gave his arm a squeeze. "Don't worry. I have some ideas that won't embarrass you. I promise."

She loved holiday shopping, and it was another trait she'd shared with her late father. Second only to Black Friday, the week before Christmas was his favorite time to go "hunting" as he'd called it. Her body picked up the vibes of the other shoppers, but she'd rarely fallen prey to the panic that could sometimes set in as the big day came closer. Today? Today she was jazzed to be shopping today with her guy.

They both wore sweaters, though she'd left the reindeer and blinking lights back at the inn in favor of a V-neck in a cranberry over her dark jeans. Zach had left his yummy leather jacket in his truck, but the navy blue cable-knit he wore with his chinos showcased those very nice shoulders. Smart man too, since the mall could get hot with so many people crammed in it.

The heels of her booties clicked over the tiled floors as she valiantly kept up with the long strides he took in his oxfords. He wasn't dressed like her Cowboy, but he still had that loose-limbed walk going on. And that delicious spicy scent.

There were some lovely boutiques in the mall, and she helped him pick out gifts for both Shannon and Carrie. Some bath giftsets from her favorite shop, a few pretty scarves and bracelets from the big department store, and then they were off to the toy store.

"Oh, look how cute!" Joy ran over to the baby dolls, looking over them to find one with red hair. "If you get one of these, Caitlyn will just love it."

"She's a little young for dolls, Joy."

Joy put her hands on her hips. "No girl is ever too young for dolls." She winked. "Or too old."

He took the doll she'd chosen and they made their way to the checkout. "Are you saying you want a doll for Christmas, Jingles?"

"No." She laughed. "Just making a point."

"Good." He squared his broad shoulders and tugged her along. "Because I've picked out something else for you."

Her heart gave a flutter. "Did you buy me something,

Cowboy?"

He nodded. "I did. And don't even think about getting it out of me."

"Fine. I got you something too, so don't go thinking you can get it out of me."

"You think I can't get you to spill?"

"Zach Harris, I think you can be downright charming when you want to be."

He looked surprised, which reminded her of the closed-off guy she'd met at Thanksgiving. Every day it got harder and harder to remember that Zach Harris. It had been so long since he was the man she was with now. The man she loved.

She tripped over her boots and stumbled into the bags Zach held.

"You okay, Jingles?"

Licking her lips, she stared up at him. "What?"

He smiled, a crooked expression that slowly stretched his sculpted lips. "Are you okay?"

She managed a nod and busied herself with righting a couple of bags that had fallen. "Sure. Fine." Holding tightly onto one bag handle, she straightened. "I mean, I'm fine."

His brow furrowed, and then he took the bags from her.

"Let's get you something to eat, baby. But not in this crowd."

The bags were loaded in the truck, the radio tuned to the Christmas carol station, but she couldn't seem to focus on anything other than the fact that she'd fallen hard for Zach Harris.

It was too soon. It was too much. It was also nothing she would share with her Cowboy. Not there at the mall. Not there in the truck.

And not there in his bed after he'd loved her so sweetly she'd had to hold back tears.

***

Zach stepped out of the Sales Center after another meeting with Ben Chapman Tuesday afternoon, feeling pretty damn good. The plans were nearly finalized and permits would be issued soon. Noah Brady would be building the structure, which would be similar in style to Billy and Shannon's farmhouse. Zach had stopped by Darby's desk in a large room the salespeople shared and she'd mentioned a few properties that might interest him in Cypress. He figured he couldn't stay at the inn forever, but did he want to think about settling here permanently like his brother and cousin had?

Thunder rumbled overhead as he made his way to where

his truck was parked on the crushed shell lot to the side of the Sales Center. A cold front was obviously moving in, and he glanced across the street. What he saw there made his belly tightened. His brother sat in the courtyard of the coffee shop with their mother. What the hell? They were having coffee together?

Holding his anger in check, he crossed the street and approached the table. Their mother was smiling down at Chase's phone as he thumbed through pictures of the baby. His pulse raced as he clenched his hands.

"Chase," he growled.

His brother started and turned, his cheeks turning red. "Hey, bro."

Helen looked up at him, wariness in her gaze. "Hello, Zachary."

Zach's lips thinned to a line. "Mom."

She winced and Chase came to his feet. "Take that stick out of your butt and sit down, bro."

"I will not."

"Damn it, Zach," Chase bit out.

He searched his brother's face, seeing worry and also anger. What the hell did Chase have to be angry about?

"Fuck this," Zach grumbled, turning away from them.

His head was pounding as he reached his truck, his breath coming fast as his chest tightened. How could Chase sit there with her? Laugh and smile with her as if she hadn't left them without one look back? He slammed his hang against the truck's hood, his eyes stinging with tears that had nothing to do with the pain radiating up his arm. Resting it on the truck's roof, he buried his face in the crook of his elbow and squeezed his eyes shut.

The skies opened then, with fat cold raindrops that pelted him. He straightened and reached for the door handle but someone gripped his shoulder, yanking him upright.

Zach spun to face them, seeing his brother.

"What the hell, Zach? Can't you even be civil to the woman?"

"Civil?" He looked around, not seeing anybody paying them much attention. That was no surprise, as anyone who lived here for any length of time got under shelter as soon as one of these winter rainstorms blew in. "I'm not having this conversation, and definitely not here."

"Why not?" Chase crossed his arms. "Why do you get to decide what we say and where?"

Still, he yanked open the truck door and got in. Chase ran around to the passenger side and then they were closed in complete privacy. Zach wrapped his hands around the steering wheel and squeezed, seeing nothing but the rain running down the windshield. He could hardly breathe now, and he sure as shit wasn't going to talk to his brother.

"She called me, Zach." Chase rubbed his hands on his thighs. "She called me and wanted to talk about Carrie and the baby."

"You couldn't say no?" Zach bit out.

"I did." Chase took in a shuddering breath. "At least, I wanted to."

"You wanted to." Zach sucked in a breath and faced his brother. "You wanted to? What the fuck does that mean?"

Chase looked down at his hands as he fidgeted. "I missed her, Zach." His voice was small and raspy. "I missed her for so damn long." He swiped at his eyes. "I said no to dinner last week. I couldn't say no now."

Anger curdled in Zach's belly as it all came rushing back. Coming home after school and calling out for her. Getting nothing but silence in return. Chase following on his heels, hope on his face too as they ran to find their father in the stables.

Wild Harry hadn't even batted an eye, hadn't hesitated one lick, before telling his young sons that their mother was gone for good. Chase had screamed at their father and run back into the house, yelling for her. Zach had just shut down.

"I missed her too," he admitted on a breath.

"Bullshit." Chase faced him, rage twisting his features. "You didn't even fucking cry, Zach. You and Harry had just gone on like nothing had changed. Like she'd never even been there at all!"

Zach had cried. He'd cried himself hoarse when nobody was around. He'd hid in the stables late at night, with only the horses to see his pain. He couldn't admit that now. He'd spent so long with that damn stiff upper lip that he couldn't tell his own brother that he'd been hurting too. He couldn't tell Chase then, and he couldn't bring himself to tell him now.

"I missed her, too," he said again.

Chase cursed, low and long. "You're just like him."

"What?" Zach lifted his head to face his brother. "What did you say?"

"You're just like that cold-hearted son-of-a-bitch. He didn't even miss her! He never talked about her and neither did you."

"What did you want me to do, Chase? I was only two years older than you."

Chase pushed his hair back from his face and glared at him. "We needed her, bro. She left us and neither you or Dad gave a crap."

Zach wouldn't argue with Chase at the moment. He couldn't find the words to convince his brother that he'd been just as devastated as he had been. He fixed an impassive expression on his face as he'd done then. It felt like a mask, but one he'd worn for so long it settled comfortably over him.

Chase cursed again. "I thought you'd change, man. I thought you'd become more open. Warmer. I was wrong."

Zach swallowed thickly, managing to raise one shoulder in a shrug.

"These past weeks since Thanksgiving, bro?" Chase said. "Since you began dating Joy? I thought you'd actually grown a fucking heart. Man, was I wrong."

Zach closed his eyes, wishing he could shut out his brother's words. Chase wasn't done, though.

"You're going to lose her." He laughed without any humor. "You're going to push her away or shut her out, and she's gonna run from you. Just like Mom did."

The rain was still falling steadily, thunder and lightning still chasing across the sky. His brother opened his door and stood, leaning down to face Zach again.

"You know what, Zach? You deserve to be all alone. Just like Harry."

Chase slammed the door and Zach finally sucked in a deep breath. His eyes were wet with hot tears, and his throat raw. He'd missed his mother, damn it. He'd longed for her on the nights he'd been sick. On the nights he'd been sad. She'd left him without a glance backwards, and he'd been alone in his grief.

Chase was right, though. He was as cold as Harry, on the outside at least. He would push Joy away with it, once the rosy glow of Christmas lights dimmed in January. She'd run from him, forget him, just like his mother had. His heart wasn't built to let someone like his Jingles inside.

He cared for her, more than he'd ever cared for another woman. Hell, he might even love her. He might have survived his mother's desertion all those years ago. When Joy inevitably left him? He'd be destroyed.

He rubbed at his eyes and stared forward again. There was only one thing to do, and he knew it. He had to end it before he ruined both of their lives.

And if he missed her? If he thought about her, craved her, forever? That would be just what he deserved.

Chapter 20

Joy shook the raindrops off of her jacket and hung it on a peg above the white wainscoting. The mudroom of the inn was just as quaint as the rest of the place, and the long benches and slate tile were tailormade for handling the mess these winter storms could bring.

Her mother was seated at the kitchen table as Joy entered, reading a magazine.

"Hi, Mom."

"Oh, Joy!" Her mother closed the magazine. "Can I talk to you for a minute?"

"I'll be right back down, Mom." Joy pushed her damp hair back from her face. "I want to talk to Zach."

"Honey…"

"See you in a minute!" Joy exited the kitchen and hurried up the curving staircase to Zach's room.

Just his suggestion, his confidence in her, was all she'd needed to explore another possibility. She'd met with the principal of the community school, just to feel her out about teaching a few art classes in the spring, and had been thrilled to find out that they needed a new teacher. She would qualify for the job, as long as she was in the process of taking a few more education classes. She also told Joy she'd be pleased if she completed her graduate degree as well, which Joy had to admit would check off another box she'd been ignoring for months now.

She knocked on Zach's door and to her surprise it swung open. "Zach?"

There was no answer, so she walked further inside. "Zach, are you here?"

The doors to the balcony were closed tight, so she figured he wasn't back from whatever he had going on at the Sales Center this afternoon. Settling down on the bed, she crossed her legs and prepared to wait.

"Joy, honey." Her mother poked her head into the room. "I have something to tell you."

"What?" At her mother's pained expression, Joy's heart tumbled to her belly. "What's wrong, Mom?"

"He left, dear. Zach checked out of the inn a couple of hours ago."

Joy blinked, trying to process what her mother was saying. "Checked out?"

A second glance around the room showed her that it no longer looked lived-in. No boots and shoes on the floor of the walk-in closet. No jackets or shirts tossed over the chair at the small table. He was pretty neat by nature, she'd learned, but he was a guy who still tended to leave a few things around.

"He left?" She slowly came to her feet, numb. "What does that mean? Where did he go?"

"I don't know, Joy." Her mother placed a hand on Joy's shoulder. "He came back from his meeting, drenched to the bone as if he'd walked the whole way, and just told me he was moving out."

Joy's heart raced now. She brushed her hair back, holding it up on her head for a second. "This doesn't make sense." She lowered her hands to her sides. "He and Chase sold the ranch. Where would he go?"

"Maybe to stay with his family?"

Joy nodded out of habit, but her mother's suggestion didn't feel quite right. Chase and Carrie were still living out at Billy's. There wouldn't be room for Zach too, would there?

"Come on downstairs, dear." Her mother put her arm around her shoulders now, leading her from the room. "I made some stew for us tonight, but your brother won't be home for dinner."

Joy nodded again, her body numb. Zach had left? He'd

moved out without any warning, and without telling her?

When they got downstairs to the kitchen, Joy snapped back to attention. "I have to find out where he went. None of this makes any sense."

Her mother's gaze skittered away and Joy's senses tingled.

"Mom, what aren't you telling me?"

Her mother sighed. "You know his mother is back, don't you?"

"I do. He was pretty torn up about it."

"Well, I have it from Lettie that…" She held up her hands. "No, I shouldn't gossip."

"What do you know?"

"It seems that Zach's brother met with their mother today."

"That makes no sense. Chase is just as angry with her as Zach."

"Not according to Lettie. They were thick as thieves today, looking at pictures of the wedding and of that darling little baby of theirs."

Joy knew it then. This had more to do with his brother than his mother. "I have to find Zach."

"I hope you find him, dear." Her mother gave her a small smile. "I think he needs you."

Joy's throat tightened. "I sure hope so."

She texted Shannon, not wanting to bother Carrie. Chase was her husband, after all. Maybe he was just as upset as Zach right now.

Shannon, is Zach there?

No.

Do you know where he is?

There was a beat as Shannon probably conferred with Billy to figure out just what she could tell Joy. Joy breathed slowly in and out as she forced herself to wait. Finally, after what felt like forever, another text came.

He's at the tent-cabin.

The tent-cabin? Joy had only been out there once, when Jessie had lived there. Carrie and Chase had lived there for a short time after their wedding, but to Joy's knowledge the place had been empty for months. At least Zach was still in Cypress Corners.

Thanks, Shannon.

Shannon sent her a little heart in return, and Joy went back into the mudroom. She slipped on her raincoat and stepped into her rubber rain boots. The terrain all around the tent-cabin was rough, as was the trail out there. After all of this rain? It would be a mess, too.

She ran out the back door toward the lot and got into the Jeep. Thank God Claire Chapman's dad had replaced the gas filter on it last week. She'd need the car for this short, muddy trip.

The tent-cabin sat at the far lakeshore, and as she made her way her wipers squeaked and slapped the raindrops away. The sound the rain made was nearly deafening on the soft roof.

She knew the place was wired for electricity, and completely livable if you didn't mind an outdoor shower and bathroom. It also had a teeny tiny kitchen tucked in one corner of the space.

She passed where the Active Adult community was being built on the right side of the main road and turned down a wet, sandy road toward the lakeshore. The tent-cabin sat beneath towering live oaks dripping with Spanish moss, and the setting was wild. Untamed. It was secluded, and it felt like it would be as good a place as any to help Zach through this mess.

His truck was parked under one thick, tall tree and she pulled the Jeep next to it. Turning off the engine, she stared out the windshield. The tent-cabin had a little wooden porch on the front of its door, but little in the way of shelter from the rain. It was blowing sideways at the moment anyway, and she doubted a full canopy would have kept her dry.

She pocketed her keys and pulled her hood back up, making a run for it. Her boots squished in the muddy sand but she made her way to the porch. Raising her hand, she ignored the rain dripping down her arm as she knocked.

There was no answer. The flaps over the windows were obviously tied down against the weather, but the structure only had one room. He had to hear her, even over the driving rain and thunder.

"Zach, I know you're in there!"

Still nothing.

"So you're going to leave me standing out in the rain, Cowboy?"

That seemed to reach him, because the door opened and he reached out to tug her inside.

"What the hell are you doing here, Joy?"

She opened her mouth to answer him, but stilled as she took in his appearance. His clothes were wrinkled, like he'd let them dry on his body, and his feet were bare. His hair was wavy and wild, and he wore a flat expression.

"Zach, I know what happened."

His brows rose, and he crossed his arms. "You do, huh?"

She flinched. His tone was beyond cold. It was downright arctic.

"You saw your brother with your mom."

His gaze sharpened, and then that flatness was back. "Doesn't matter. She left once. She'll leave again."

She ached to hold him close. To comfort the abandoned little boy he hid inside, but she knew he wouldn't let her. He was self-sufficient, which was due in part to his mother but also to his father. From what she'd heard, Wild Harry Harris had little to do with either of his sons as they'd grown up.

She curled her hands into fists to keep from touching him. "Zach, that doesn't matter." She sucked in a breath. "Does it?"

"Jingles, you don't get it. Everybody leaves."

Her belly clenched. "Everybody?"

"My father might have been there, but inside he was gone. You'll leave too, so it might as well be now."

She pulled back. "What?"

"Go, Joy." He turned from her, his body held stiffly. "Just, go."

Who was this guy? This wasn't the guy who'd made that awkward declaration that had thrilled her to her toes. The guy who wanted to be exclusively hers, and demanded she be the same for him. This was still the guy she loved, though. And her heart felt torn in pieces as she stared at his rigid back.

"Zach…"

"We're done," he said, his voice low. "Better now than later."

Tears stung at the back of her eyes, then spilled over her lashes. "Zach, please."

He said nothing more. She stood there, dripping rain over the tent-cabin's wood planked floor as her tears continued to stream down her cheeks. This was it. She felt it. He ended it because he thought she would leave.

Turning away from him, she stepped back out into the storm and got back into the Jeep. Then she sobbed loud and long until her throat was sore.

***

Zach covered his face with his hands, groaning as the truth hit him square in the belly. He'd done it. He'd broken any ties with his Jingles.

After a long time, he heard her Jeep start up. She was gone. Just like he'd dreaded. Just like he'd wanted.

"It's for the best." He grunted. "Shit, that's just what Harry said when she left."

He sank down on the edge of the iron bed and folded his hands. It was clear why Chase and Carrie had outgrown this place, and also clear why it was nicknamed the love shack. It was simply furnished, with the big iron bed with an old-fashioned quilt spread over it. Small kitchen, and not much else, and that was it.

He hadn't bothered trying to reach his brother after their fight, and wouldn't now. Billy had the keys to this place, thank God, so he'd just driven to their place after leaving the inn. If Chase had been there, he didn't know. Or care, right now. Chase could go to Hell, after all he'd said.

Zach flopped back onto the bed. Of course Chase would think he hadn't cried at all. He sure as hell didn't let anything show after their mother left. God, he *was* just like their father.

Wiping a hand over his face, he ignored the dampness that came away. He scrubbed his hands over his thighs, came to his feet, and then crossed to his duffel bag. Reaching inside, he found the jewelry box he'd tucked in there. Opening it, he looked at the delicate jingle bell he'd bought for his girl. When she was his girl, anyway.

He set it down on the table and went to the little fridge set under one window flap. There were a couple of beers in there, like Billy had said when he'd handed him the key. He was a good guy, his cousin. Better than he was. That was for sure.

Cracking open a bottle, he sat in one of the small chairs and drank.

In the morning he felt like he'd been ridden hard and put away wet. The storm had passed, like they always seemed to do this time of the year. One look out of a window showed him clear skies. He grabbed a few things out of his duffel and stepped into his work boots for the trek out to the shower. He felt a little bit better after, but the hollow feeling in his belly wouldn't go away.

He'd have to find a place to live, and sooner rather than later. He sure as hell wouldn't settle out here. Never mind the chance of running into his mother. He'd be sure to see Joy, his Jingles, and not be able to be with her. Not be able to talk to her without screwing everything up again. A cold, clean break. That was what this was, and what he needed.

He was dressed and just running a comb through his damp hair when a knock came at the door.

"Don't do this to me, Jingles," he muttered as he all but dragged himself over to the door.

He took a breath and pulled open the door, shocked to find his mother standing there.

Chapter 21

She looked so small. Almost delicate, if you ignored the determination on her face. Anger simmered in his gut, but he managed to keep himself from slamming the door on her.

"What do you want?" he bit out.

She squared her shoulders. "I have to speak with you, Zachary."

"I don't think so."

"I do." She crossed her arms, mimicking his stance. "Are you going to let me in?" When he hesitated she clicked her tongue. "I know Harry raised you to have manners."

He stepped back and she took a few steps inside.

"This place is very quaint." She trailed her fingers over the iron footboard of the bed. "I can see why Chase and Carrie lived here for a while."

He just shut the door, beyond pissed at this woman.

"We need to talk, son."

He stiffened. "Don't call me that."

Her eyes, his own eyes really, welled up with tears but she didn't seem like she would try to use them against him. Now yet, anyway.

"I deserve that, Zachary." She sighed. "That and so much

more."

She perched on the edge of the bed so he sat as far away as he could in the small room. He took a chair in the kitchen again, fiddling with the bottlecaps from the four empty bottles set on the table.

"I'm so sorry I left the way I did."

"The way you did?" He glanced over at her. "Just what the hell does that mean?"

"Your father and I… We just weren't meant for each other."

She took off her jacket and tugged on the sleeves of her sweater. He remembered that habit of hers, and shoved the memory aside. He couldn't speak at the moment, anger and hurt tightening his chest.

"No, that's not quite right," she went on. "I couldn't be what he needed."

"What about what I needed?" He swallowed thickly. "What Chase needed?"

She looked him square in the eye as she slowly shook her head. "I wasn't a good mother. Not at the end."

"You didn't just leave Harry." He shook his head. "You left your sons."

"I was miserably unhappy, Zachary."

"It was all about you, then? Did you even think about us, Mom?" He held up one hand. "Never mind. Don't answer that. You'll just say what you think I want to hear."

"I know you might not believe me, but I've regretted it every day since."

"We never knew it on our end."

She nodded again, looking down at her clasped hands. She'd aged. He could see that now, but she was still the pretty mother he'd loved so hard when he was a kid.

"Why now?"

She lifted her head. "What?"

"Why come back now?"

"I saw your father had passed, and I didn't want to wait any longer." She took in a shuddering breath. "I wanted to get to know you all again."

"How could you just leave?" He heard it in his own voice, that little boy asking for his mother to fix his boo-boos. "Was it because of me?"

She gaped at him, her eyes opened wide. "Oh no, Zachary. Why would you think that?"

"Because of all the help I needed." He swallowed. "The

reading we had to do every night."

To his amazement, she smiled. "I loved helping you with your reading. It was the one time I felt like a real mother, other than when I had to patch up you and your brother's bumps and scrapes."

Zach choked up a little, so he just gave a short nod. "That's good to hear." He cleared his throat. "Thanks."

She rose and approached him, and then placed a hand on his shoulder. He didn't shrug it off, but he still stiffened.

"Zachary, you're a good man."

He looked her square in the eye. "No. I'm not. I'm just like him."

"No, son." She winced. "Sorry. No, you're not."

"I'm cold like him, Mom."

"Chase told you that."

"He told you he said that?"

"He did, and he felt awful. Especially when I told him how wrong he was."

"How can you say that?" Zach had to know. "How do you know I'm not like him?"

"I see you, Zachary. You're torn up about that possibility. Your father, God rest his soul, wouldn't have given a fig in a field about it."

"Fig in a field?" Zach smiled a little. "I remember you used to say that all the time. Never heard anybody else say it. Not before and not since."

She shrugged and also gave him a small smile. "I'm glad you have those memories. I wish I could go back and give you boys as many memories as I have of you two."

Recollections slammed through him, of his mother helping him with so much patience as he stumbled his way through his reading homework. Making him feel better when he had the chicken pox, and then caring for both him and Chase and working hard to distract them from scratching those itching bumps.

"You're a good mother," Zach said. "At least, you were."

She nodded with obvious resignation. "Thank you. And believe me, I know. I lost out on so much."

He sniffed and squared his shoulders. "Did you get to see the little carrottop in person?"

A smile broke out over her face. "Oh my, she's adorable! She has so much of Chase in her, but enough of that pretty Carrie too."

Zach nodded. "She's something, all right."

"Your brother feels awful about what he said, Zach."

"He thinks I didn't cry." He snorted. "Hell, I cried buckets after you left."

"I'm so sorry."

She reached down to hug him and he grabbed her to him. It had been so long since he'd felt his mother's hugs.

"I know I can't make it up to you both," she said. "But I'm still going to try. If you'll let me."

"I'll try," he rasped. He squeezed his eyes shut as he recalled how he'd treated Joy last night. "Shit, I'm an idiot."

She straightened and touched his cheek. "What are you talking about?"

"I told Joy… God, I can't even think about what I said to her."

His mother nodded. "Lettie Fairfax told me all about your girlfriend." At Zach's raised brow she shrugged. "I'm your mother, Zachary. I wanted to know about this girl."

"She's amazing, Mom." He stood and began to pace. "She came out here last night. She'd heard about my fight with Chase and was worried about me."

"She sounds like a nice girl."

"She's a nice girl, but more than that. She's funny and

sweet and smart. And talented. You should see the silhouettes she did at the festival."

"I did. Carrie showed me the one of her and little Caitlyn."

"She came here and I sent her away. Just like that."

"Does she know you love her?"

"What?" He turned to face her, stunned. "I love her?"

"Are you asking me?" She smiled and held up the jingle bell necklace. "Seems to me like you do. Do you miss her?"

He reached out and closed his hand around the bell. "Like there's a hole in my belly."

"Would you miss her if you lost her?"

The prospect sent a stab of pain through him. "I would."

She grinned at him. "You see?"

"Again, what?"

"You're nothing like your father, Zachary. You're not cold."

"I'm not." He thought for a second. "I'm not, but I'm an idiot. What if I can't fix this?"

"Go." She headed for the door. "Go and tell her how you feel, Zachary. You'll regret it if you don't."

She left him to his thoughts, which was probably her intention. They weren't tight again, but that might happen over time. Doesn't it heal all wounds? Joy would say something like that, right before bursting into some Christmas song. Damn, he missed her.

He might have been a dick last night, but he wasn't going to be the fool his father was. He unclenched his fist and looked at the bell resting in his palm.

He'd made a mistake. That was true. And now he would do everything he had to do to fix it.

***

Joy smiled at the family posed for their photo op.

"Why isn't Santa here?" one of the kids asked.

For what felt like the hundredth time, Joy answered this question. "Santa has to get ready for his big night. Tonight is Christmas Eve, you know."

Most all of the people seemed to buy her excuse. This would be the last time they held sittings anyway. Tonight would be a whole new level of discomfort for her. The inn would host its annual Christmas Eve dinner, and they expected a full house. It was an open invitation, but RSVPs were appreciated. Or so she'd seen printed on every announcement she'd sent out last week. Funny thing, but when she'd mailed all of them she'd been happily anticipating spending the evening with Zach. In his arms. Under the mistletoe. Making Christmas wishes that would continue into the New Year. Now she was just any other single sad sack, staring down the barrel of a long, lonely winter.

"I think that's it, sis."

Tom's voice was hesitant, which was beginning to really get on her nerves. Everybody seemed to be treating her like a charity case. Like Tiny Tim just sitting all alone on a little stool by the fireplace.

"Thanks."

She didn't even make eye contact, but just clicked through the photos on the camera he handed her. Out of the corner of her eye she watched him hesitate until he finally left her the heck alone.

"Joy?" Her sister Becky came into the parlor, concern clear on her face. "Do you need anything?"

"What?" She turned to Becky. "Do I need anything? To what, mend my stupid broken heart?"

Becky blinked. "I was talking about the party, but okay."

Joy blew out a breath. "I'm sorry, Becky. I'm just tired of all of the pitying looks I'm getting all over Cypress over the past few days."

"So you broke up with him."

"Is that a question? If it is, no. I didn't."

"He broke up with you?" Becky grunted. "What a dick."

Joy closed her laptop and faced her. "No, he's not a dick. He ended things, Becky. Nothing I could say now will convince him that I won't leave."

"Leave? Why would he think that?"

Joy wanted to tell her sister everything, but it wasn't her secret to share. Zach was all twisted up over his mother's desertion. If he couldn't see his own way out of it, talking it out with somebody else wouldn't make it any better.

"I'm not going to be his relationship tutor, Becky. He thinks what he thinks, and he's as stubborn as one of his cows." She found a smile as she nearly heard him correct her. "Cattle."

Becky hugged her, then gave her shoulder a pat. "Let's go get ready for this party, then. The Rollins girls are both free now. Why not make all of them see what they're missing?"

"If you say so. Wait. Who's missing what, exactly?"

Becky's cheeks turned pink but she shook her head. "Nobody in particular."

"Hmm. You're lucky my love life is such a mess right now, sis. Otherwise I'd ply you with spiked eggnog until you spilled."

Becky wove her arm through Joy's and led her upstairs. "Okay, but I still think that eggnog sounds like a pretty good idea. Ooh, or maybe Mom's holiday punch?"

"Now you're talking."

In the end, Joy made the decision to sip slowly at her cup of punch. True to its name, it could pack a wallop. It was spiced, though. And went really well with the peppermint cookie in her hand.

She stood in the dining room, which was the main party area tonight. The doors were all open to the balcony, and standing heaters were lit and placed strategically to keep the outdoor space nearly as warm as the indoor. It was crowded, and through those doors she saw that Lettie held court at one of the tables. She was dressed to the nines, or so she'd told Joy when she'd arrived. The woman did look good, even if her sharp eyes had run over Joy with more concern than she wanted right now.

The Chapmans came in, or nearly all of them did, at once. She spoke to Harmony and Tammy, joked around with Nick and tickled little Raffaella, and avoided any mention of working with Billy and Zach at the stables. It was too much to get into, and she wouldn't ruin the party. Her own holiday might suck the big candy cane, but she would just keep that tucked in her own stocking.

"Hey, Joy." Shannon Harris walked over to her. "How are you doing tonight?"

Joy brightened, putting on a smile at least a little bit due to the punch. "I'm good. You?"

Shannon bit her lip, and then shrugged. "We're good."

She searched Joy's face for something, but Joy just lifted her chin. "I'm fine, Shannon. I promise."

"Fine." Shannon laughed lightly. "If you say so."

Joy knew that Shannon was different from her sister Jessie, despite how identical they appeared. Jessie was a Pixie and Shannon was more of a Nymph. She had this whole mysterious thing going on, and if Joy was in a more accommodating mood she might participate in the guessing game the woman was playing.

Carrie came over to say hello as well, bringing Zach and Chase's mother along with them. Helen Snow was dressed a lot like Lettie, if a little more subdued.

"Hello, Joy," Helen said.

"Hello."

"You look lovely."

Joy accepted the compliment with a nod. She did look

good. Her sister had made sure of it. Tonight Joy wore a pretty red sweater, not the kind with twinkly lights, reindeer or snowflakes but the kind that showed off her curves, and a short black leather skirt. High boots seemed to be required too, and Joy had agreed. Her hair was in loose waves and she'd actually taken time with her makeup. It was sad, but right now the outfit felt more like dress-up than her outrageous elf costume had.

Carrie and her mother-in-law began to talk about the holiday decorations and the spread of appetizers, not to mention the delicious and potent eggnog.

She felt the change in the air before she saw him. It was inevitable. His entire family was here already, and even though she'd wished he would stay away it seemed this one wouldn't come true either. It also sucked that their connection hadn't lessened, no matter how much he wanted it to. Did she? She took another sip of punch and steeled herself. She had to, didn't she?

Turning her head a notch, she watched him walk in. Oh, he looked so good. She hadn't seen him in days, but even objectively he looked amazing. Long legs clad in chinos. A fisherman sweater in a yummy oatmeal color. His black leather jacket hanging on him just right. His hair was relatively tamed and his eyes searched the room. Was he looking for her? Did he think she'd take the coward's way out and avoid her own family's party?

He spotted her and there was no escaping. His family looked on, and wasn't that adding insult to injury, as he drew closer.

"Jingles."

That silly nickname! Just that one word in his deep rumbly voice and she was ready to beg him to rethink this whole thing.

"Hello." She'd put as much chill in her voice as she could manage, yet it still came out breathy. Needy. "I'm surprised to see you here."

He stepped closer and she could smell him. *Darn it.*

"I have to talk to you," he said.

She crossed her arms, affecting a strength she didn't feel. "You have nothing to say that I want to hear."

"I was wrong."

She blinked. "Go on."

He gave her that slow smile that made her insides melt like hot chocolate. "Jingles, I was wrong. I know now that you won't ever leave me."

Could he read her mind? She was never very good at hiding her feelings, and she'd never really tried around him anyway.

"How…how do you know?" she needed to know.

He took her hand in his, holding it over his heart. "Because you're in here, baby."

"Darn it," she murmured, dropping her chin. "You went and made me want to cry."

"Don't cry." He put his finger under her chin and lifted her face to his. "Kiss me."

She licked her lips. "Kiss you?"

He nodded, his eyes going skyward. She looked up and saw the mistletoe. Throwing her arms around his neck, she kissed him with everything she had. His arms encircled her, and as he kissed her back she heard the laughs and claps spread through the dining room.

She pulled slightly away to find him grinning. "Let's take this upstairs, Jingles."

She nodded and he took her hand, pulling her along as they hurried through the crowd and up the stairs to her little room. Once they were tucked inside, he pulled her to him.

"I'm so damned sorry, baby." He buried his face in her neck, shaking a little as he kissed the side of her throat. "I was wrong, and I'm sorry."

She caught his head and urged him to look at her. "What happened to change your mind?"

He kissed her, then caressed her cheek. "My mother came to see me."

"You're kidding."

He shook his head. "She told me why she left, but it wasn't like she was making any excuses. She feels terrible about all the time she's missed."

"I can imagine."

"And she told me I'm not like my father."

"Is that what Chase told you?"

"Easy, Jingles. Before you go telling off my brother, he feels bad too." He grinned. "He was even more wrong than I was."

Her heart thumped and her breath caught. "What do you mean?"

"I'm not cold, Joy. I'm not closed off, and I would miss the hell out of you if I had to go on without you for the rest of my life."

"The rest of your life?"

He nodded. "Yep. I love you, Joy."

She bit her lip, blinking as tears blurred her vision. "Oh,

Cowboy."

"Then you forgive me?"

"Yes!" She hugged him so tight until he lifted her in his arms. "Yes, Zach. I love you, too!"

"Ah, Jingles."

He kissed her again and she knew in her heart what she'd wanted all along. This man. This love. Zach was the wish she hadn't dared make when this whole thing started.

She pulled back and looked into his gorgeous blue eyes.

"Merry Christmas, Cowboy."

Epilogue

"You clean up nice, Cowboy."

Zach winked at her as he straightened his tie. "I have to look at least half as good as my girl."

Joy leaned up to kiss him just because she could. He looked more than nice, and the expression in his eyes was even nicer. He no longer looked sad. Lost. Angry.

They'd been living in the tent-cabin since Christmas Day, and it had been a little challenging to both get dressed for tonight's New Year's Eve party. It would be held at the Clubhouse, the upscale club and restaurant in Cypress Corners, and just about everyone they knew would be there.

She smoothed her hands over her short dress. It was silver and sparkly and just right for a New Year's Eve party, and the strappy heels she'd bought at a boutique in Orlando were fun and pretty. Nothing was prettier than the silver filigree jingle bell hanging from the necklace Zach had given her for Christmas, though. It jingled softly as she finished getting ready.

"Your brother and Carrie will be there." She put on her lip gloss and fluffed out her waves. "And probably your mother."

"I know." Zach shrugged on his suit jacket as she eyed him in the small mirror. He rocked the polished look as well as he did the rough rancher. "She told me."

"She did?" Joy turned back to him. "When?"

"Yesterday." He gave her a small smile. "I met her for coffee."

"You did, huh?"

"You were right, Jingles." He leaned against the small table in the kitchen and crossed his arms. "I have to give her a chance to be in my life."

"You don't have to, but you'll be happier for it." She walked over to him and wrapped her arms around his waist. "And a happy guy makes for a happy girl."

He crinkled his nose at her, and then chuckled. "How can you still have so much Christmas spirit? And not a candy cane in sight."

"This isn't Christmas spirit, Zach." She nuzzled the hollow of his neck, drawing his scent into herself until she sighed. "This is happiness. Pure and simple."

He held her close and she curled into him. She would never get tired of being in his arms, and since Christmas Eve she'd barely been anywhere but.

"How about we skip this party, Cowboy?"

He snorted. "After all you said about mending fences?"

She leaned back and looked up at him. "Oh, don't pull that ranch talk on me. You and Chase will be fine."

"You're right." He winked. "We're going to watch the games together tomorrow."

She clasped her hands. "You see!"

"Yep. Hard not to." He pocketed his wallet and tugged on the sleeves of his jacket. "Did you figure out when you start at the school?"

"When the kids come back from break, they'll have a new art teacher."

He let out a whoop and hugged her close. "I knew it would work out."

She laughed. "Since when are you so optimistic?"

"Since picking up a sexy little elf on the side of the road."

He reminded her of that often, as if she needed him to. What had started out as the worst day of her life had turned swiftly to her best. "Still waters, Zach." She touched his smoothly shaven jaw. "That's what you are."

"So you always say. How about you tell me what you got me for Christmas? It's been almost a week, Jingles. People are beginning to talk."

She waited a beat, and then reached under the bed for the

package she'd hidden there.

"Seriously?" He laughed. "It was there the whole time?"

"Not the whole time. I had to put on some finishing touches." She handed it to him, hardly able to wait for him to see it now. "Open it."

He hefted it in his hands, and then tore the off the red sparkly tissue paper. Laughing again, he turned the wide wooden oval upright. "Cypress Corners Stables," he read. "Cowpokes Welcome." He held it close. "Jingles, this is perfect."

"I'm so glad you like it. I know it's a little corny."

"It's perfect."

"I got the best present Christmas Eve, Zach. You." She fingered her necklace. "And this, of course."

"There's no denying that." He placed the sign on the table and faced her again. "Now how about you tell me your Christmas wish?"

"You're not wearing your Santa suit."

"Are you getting kinky on me, Jingles?"

"You sure are something, Zach Harris."

"Nah. I'm just the guy who loves you. Forever."

She blinked back the tears when they threatened. "Forever?"

He nodded. "That okay?"

She felt all light and tingly inside, like a just-popped bottle of champagne.

"Cowboy, that's just what I wished for."

About the Author

JoMarie DeGioia is a bestselling author of Historical and Contemporary Romance. She's known Mickey Mouse from the "inside," has been a copyeditor for her tiny town's newspaper, and a bookseller. She is the author of over 40 Romances, and writes Young Adult Fantasy/Adventure stories and Paranormal Romance too. She gets lost in DIY projects around the house and works out plot ideas during long runs. She divides her time between Central Florida and New England.

Discover other books by JoMarie DeGioia

The Gentlemen Undercover series, including

A Hero and a Gentleman

The Shopgirls of Bond Street series, including

That Determined Mister Latham

The Dashing Nobles series, including

More Than Passion

Pride and Fire

Just Perfect

More Than Charming

The Gentlemen Undercover series, including

A Hero and a Gentleman

The Cypress Corners series, including

Cypress Corners Boxed Set

Finding Harmony

Taming Jake

Loving Cassie

Winning Ben

Showing Jessie

Seeing Shannon (Barefoot Bay Kindle Worlds Novella)

Dreaming Eli

Giving Chase (Barefoot Bay Kindle Worlds Novella)

Kissing Bree

Wishing Joy

The Gifted YA Fantasy/Adventure Trilogy, including

Gifted

Braunachs of the Dell series, including

Luke's Gold

Patrick's Promise

Connect with me online

Twitter: https://twitter.com/JoMarieDeGioia

Facebook:

https://www.facebook.com/JoMarie.DeGioia.Author

Website: www.jomariedegioia.com